DANCE

DANCE

BABY

DANCE

TANZANIA GLOVER

TANZANIA GLOVER

DANCE DANCE BABY DANCE

Cover Art by Dionne Richard

TANZANIA GLOVER

www.tanzaniaglover.com

Booking With Love
332 S Michigan Ave
Suite #121- 2217
Chicago, IL 60604
www.bookingwithlove.com

DANCE DANCE BABY DANCE

To my favorite overthinker and best friend Dionne, I'll never forget the day we plotted this whole book out. Thank you for always listening and being there for me even when it hurts sometimes. No matter what I promise to always return the favor.

DANCING WITH THE STARS

Lessons in life will be repeated until they are learned. -Frank Sonnenberg

Last year when I met Theo Smith at his concert, the only thing I was looking for in a relationship was a way out of one. My name wasn't Aaliyah, but I was still just one in a million when it came to all the women and teenaged girls in the arena that night vying for his attention too. I had a slight leg up though

DANCE DANCE BABY DANCE

since not only was I front row and center, but I'd also been invited by the man we were all there to see.

Now I had never chased a nigga a day in my life, but when I saw one I wanted I knew exactly how to put myself in his line of vision to then *be chased*. Or at least I thought I'd known how because it damn near took a Goodyear blimp and ten attempts before I finally got his attention from going viral dancing to one of his songs.

I'd been dancing since before I could walk and getting paid to do it for years at that point because sharing clips from the classes I taught gained me a big following. All press wasn't good press though because I got trolled like every other plus-sized woman who dared to exist let alone exist confidently on the internet.

And while I did my best to never judge people by their looks, I couldn't help but notice it was always the folks who could only be described as aggressively average that had something to say about my weight. But what made it worse sometimes was that a lot of the calls were coming from inside the house.

And it hurt so much worse when some of my fellow big girl baddies would falsely accuse me of trying to abandon them every time I naturally dropped a few pounds from being more active on tour. Too big for some and not big enough for others was the story of my life though and after a while I gave up on giving a fuck. My body wasn't anybody's business but my own and I had never wanted to be anybody's Great Fat Hope™ anyway.

I just wanted to be Tempest.

And that night all Tempest wanted to be was somebody who could say that she had fucked Theo Smith.

Just once.

Back when I'd first been put on to his music he had just been a cutie on the come up, but his glow up had been one for the books. He went from looking like a choir boy who would rather die than steal from the collection plate to '90s fine overnight. I'm talking ain't never stepped foot on a college campus but still got a degree in Fine Arts *fine*!

And when his locs started to grow out and frame his beautiful face? Baby it was a wrap for me even though it shouldn't have been. Because while we didn't have too big of an age gap, it was still enough for pause on my end so I knew it could never be anything other than a fun little link up...if it ever actually even happened in the first place.

And then came concert night when the stars and his baby sister/assistant DeeDee had finally aligned for us to meet. I'd been so nervous that I almost didn't respond to her, but him following me and liking literally everything I posted after told me that I was on his mind too.

Not caring about any of the opening acts allowed me to take my time getting ready for him, already knowing it would be a night to remember. And of course I was right but not for the reasons I would've thought.

TANZANIA GLOVER

Still relatively fresh from a bad car wreck, Theo managed to put on a bomb comeback show and even surprised me by taking time out of his set to say thanks for helping get him his first number one song. I ended up thanking him though after he'd teasingly dared me to come on stage during one of my favorite parts of his show.

Usually he would choose some shy, wallflower type of fan that he would completely ravage up there, but for my turn I turned the tables and handcuffed him in the hot seat. The first thing I noticed was just how good he was at maintaining eye contact.

DANCE DANCE BABY DANCE

Because in the few minutes I was on stage he might've blinked thrice, outright refusing to take his eyes off me any longer than he absolutely had to.

That's when I knew for sure he was on the same type of time I was on and what started off as a dance between two people who knew how to put on a show, left him bruising his wrists trying to get free to put his hands on me. Preparedness had met opportunity in the best way and I was sure I had him.

Or again at least I thought I'd had him until boom in came his ex Natalie backstage after the curtains had closed. I would have loved to pretend that I didn't know who she was, but even casual fans of Theo knew her since most of his early songs were about their little high school puppy love relationship.

Now from my point of view, and yes I had been watching hard, they seemed to be more off than on, but her presence that night let me know he was still off limits. And a real bummer it was because the Tweety bird in me was fluttering hard to get out of her cage. but ultimately it wasn't the end of the world so I just took my horny ass home and tried to forget about the night that could have been with me and Mr. Smith.

DANCE DANCE BABY DANCE

The internet decided to remind me every day after though once the video of me dancing for him on stage went viral too. It was cute, but aside from repeatedly seeing his spellbound face on my timeline that next week from tags, I'd assumed that the opportunity had come and gone, but he had other plans and decided that he would show up to my Friday night dance class.

Now this time around I knew I would need a stronger adjective than nervous because every species of butterfly was in my stomach fluttering right alongside Tweety, but I kept it as cute as possible and tried to teach like usual even though I felt his eyes on me the whole time. It was the same way he'd fixated on me at his show, but this time he was acting even more single than before and not trying to hide his motives at all.

As expected when class was dismissed he stayed behind for some *extra help* and he was very close to getting it after I'd misplaced my mind for a minute, but unfortunately for him I found it when we were interrupted and I came back to my senses. I had always been a girl's girl so celebrity crush or not I knew I couldn't go through with it even though I wrestled with my thoughts that entire night after he swore that they were broken up for good that time.

To my surprise he had actually been telling the truth though because after that he began a relentless campaign to get me in his next video, on his tour and in his bed. I agreed to the first two without much fanfare, but when I realized I was starting to like him more than I should have I knew I would be better off acting like *his* celebrity crush Janet Jackson and making him wait awhile.

Like I'd said I was still hotel AC cool on anything serious, but yeah he was definitely saying and doing all the right things and I figured he would be a nice little starter for my summer roster. Plus lie and say I was the only young ratchet who pre Korrine Stephans dreamed of being a lead video vixen.

I had already been cemented in hoochie mama history from being in the backgrounds plenty of times before because the casting folks always knew who to call when they wanted some real good-googly-moogly, juicy twerking, but the actual leading lady? Nope. That was a vision that only Theo could see.

DANCE DANCE BABY DANCE

And while I was positive it was just to get him closer to some cootie cat at that point, he still went above, beyond and out of his way to stand up for me on the shoot and make me feel comfortable. That act alone had pulled my panties down, but I gladly stepped out of them on my own after he managed to plan the most thoughtful and romantic date I'd ever been on.

Off rip I knew having sex with Theo would be well worth the body, but what I wasn't expecting was just how emotional and vulnerable the whole experience would turn out to be. Because before I even knew what'd really led to it I was crying and sharing *take it to the grave* type secrets while he made me promises that sounded good, but we were both unsure if he would actually keep them.

Or maybe it'd just been me who was unsure because when we got back from the shoot in Las Vegas to life as usual in LA, he did the unthinkable. He did exactly what he said he would and he kept showing up for me. For us. In one fell swoop he put my Hot Girl Summer™ on ice and I swear neither one of us ever looked back.

Dancing on his tongue so often had me questioning if it was

really the beginning of a new love story or just an extended version of the joyride I'd initially wanted, but either way I wasn't getting off anytime soon. Because I deserved something good and I decided that I would stick around as long as it felt that way.

I had been there once before though and the beginning was nothing but butterflies and lies so I watched him for small things, the shit that I had missed or just plain ignored in my previous serious relationship. I loved that aside from keeping me bent over that he didn't act any differently when we were alone and most importantly he never tried to isolate me.

He was genuinely interested in getting to know all my dance friends and family and bringing me around his too. But I knew my feelings were real for real when I started seeing him with my eyes closed then being happy he was still there when I opened them. Plus Theodore had always been my favorite chipmunk anyway so boom we were clearly meant to be together, right?

His little mean ass fans thought otherwise though and they were not shy about letting it be known that they would rather see him with literally anybody but my "old fat ass". Because unlike back in the day when male singers had to pretend to be single, nowadays you could have a girl, but it couldn't be just any girl. It had to be the *right* girl. Relatable enough to feel like they too could one day get chosen but still somebody to aspire to.

And since I had aged out of his target demo years ago I wasn't too surprised by the response, but the level of backlash became high enough to make me uncomfortable being public with him. Because ultimately I knew cursing out little girls half my age wouldn't be the move especially since life, hormones, kids and stress would eventually humble them better than I ever could.

Even at my tiniest though I had never been the toothpick I needed to be for the ballerina dreams my family had for me, but I was still very small for my height only it definitely wasn't natural or for the right reasons. I did a lot of unhealthy shit to make weight, but it was the strangest thing because as hard as I was on myself then and as much as I sacrificed I still didn't even really like my body.

All of that felt like a different lifetime now though because my post ballet days of wishing I was thick like video girls more than caught up to me by the time I was diagnosed with PCOS in my early twenties. But no matter what size I found myself at these days I would never go back to beating up on my body especially since I had finally found somebody who loved it even more than I did.

Unfortunately I had seen men look at me with lust in their eyes even before hitting puberty, but there was something else besides that coming from Theo. It was like I had bedazzled him and made him incapable of focusing on anything or anybody else if I was around and let him tell it, it was even worse when I was gone.

Choirboy was sprung.

In fact he was so sprung that the thought of me being away from him was what had led to our first argument about six months in. Well that and me not telling him that I'd been auditioning to work with another singer behind his back, but in my defense it wasn't just any ol' body. It was THEE Bianca King and nobody in their right mind would have expected me to pass up an opportunity that big.

But Theo hadn't been in his right mind. He was in love. And even though he had shown his **entire** ass acting out for the last few dates of his fall tour, I'm talking interior and exterior, the way we had bounced back from that situation and put in work learning to communicate better told me that we really might've had it in us to make it last.

But old habits never did die softly, did they? In fact the little motherfuckers always seemed to die rough and hard so *of course* I had been keeping another secret from him.

Anybody with eyes could see that I had to dodge dicks daily so I wouldn't even have been offended if the assumption was that I had maybe stepped out on Theo while I was out on the European leg of Bianca King's Revival World Tour. I mean even

he had been booking me separate
hotel rooms, claiming he didn't
like the thought of me sharing a
cramped space even though he
knew it was tour culture and
thugging it out together was what
built camaraderie.

*Baby I swear my phone is
desert dry*

*Nah tell that to somebody who
don't know how wet it can get*

But ultimately he should
have known there was nothing to
worry about since I was
notoriously reserved as fuck until
you got me drunk or dancing or
worse drunk *and* dancing and
except for performing I hadn't
been doing either lately. Because

while everybody else was sneaking out and galivanting in each historic Flour Ranger city, I'd been mostly staying in and counting the days until I could see him again.

In the middle of making up last year I'd figured he was just saying whatever it took to get me back, but he'd clearly meant it when he told me that he would follow me anywhere because so far he'd been doing just that. For the entirety of the tour he had already planned to come be with me whenever his schedule allowed which was honestly more often than I would have expected.

But I guess I shouldn't have been too surprised since I'd known he was a goner when he started sucking my toes on the regular. Because a massage after a long day was one thing, but baby more than a decade of ballet then another of dancing in heels had done me dirty in the foot department so you wouldn't ever catch me outside with exposed toes. But the way Theo kept them in his mouth and sucked on them every chance he got you would've thought they were the last neckbone in the pot.

At the moment they were aching bad for his warm lips as I waited for him to come rescue me

DANCE DANCE BABY DANCE

from fugazi ass France, surprisingly the least exciting place we'd been all tour. But I guess I couldn't blame all my boredom on the lackluster cities since being able to throw back a cold one to celebrate a good show or just enjoying a nice glass of wine over a meal would have for sure made things more bearable.

But I could barely even keep crackers down lately and the smell of just about everything made me nauseous. Yeah it was pretty obvious and overwhelming what was going on so I didn't exactly need Steve or Blue to pick up the clues for me. And because even though the balcony to my room overlooked the beautiful Saint-Denis canal, I'd still clearly been living in the river of denial since finding out that I, Tempest Anita Randall, was indeed with child.

You been lettin' somebody touch your ladybug, ain't you?

I almost smiled to myself after hearing my paternal grandmother Teenie's words bounce around in my head. Lord knows that woman had been warning me about running around with boys all my life, but she had still been the one to give me my first condoms to prevent the very situation I'd found myself in. The lesson of the day was to always listen to Teenie.

"Granma, why they call you Teenie and you so big?" I had asked as a messy ass kid trying to get her riled up and cussin' how I liked her since my parents tried their hardest not to around me.

"I look like a damn Ruth to you?" she'd responded with obvious contempt for her government name.

But she hadn't looked like a *Teenie* either though which had been the whole point of the question. I later learned from older pictures that once upon a time she had been a teenie tiny little thing and the name had just naturally come with the body.

The message that suddenly appeared on my phone's darkened screen made me tuck away all the fond memories back close to my heart where they were safe. The sender was exactly who I'd expected, my co-conspirator Theo Thee Sperminator, letting me know he'd landed and that he was officially a nigga in Paris.

"What you got on? Send me a pic," he asked like there was still an ocean between us and not just baggage claim and an Uber.

"Mm mn. I'm already in bed and I'm not about to get oiled up," I declined since I wasn't in the

mood to look like a warmed up honeybun for him tonight.

"Well I miss you so I'll take an ashy one just this once," he joked knowing how serious I was about my nudes. I always swore that if they ever leaked it would become a national holiday because nobody would ever be able to say my shit wasn't on fleek, da fuck.

He had been teasing me for days about going through Paris syndrome and promising to bring the fun with him when he arrived, but I wasn't sure anything could save it after I had finally gotten my suspicions confirmed.

For the last two weeks I had allowed myself to pretend like the potential Theo sponsored bean growing inside my body wasn't real and focused on just making it to Paris. Because according to Teenie Paris was supposed to make everything okay.

My entire childhood she had told me all these fantastical ass tales about how dancing under Parisian lights had changed her life, but so far the whole trip had been a dud from the surprisingly flavorless food to their cheap asses not even lighting up the damn Eiffel Tower all night.

Literally if you blinked you could miss it and I had been

missing it for the past two nights since I went to bed as soon as I got in from the show run-throughs. But now that I had woken up and could probably catch a quick glimpse I wasn't even interested anymore since I had more pressing things to get to.

The right thing to do would've been to tell Theo about the baby so we could deal with the matter together, the same way we had created it....but then I thought that maybe face down ass up wasn't really appropriate for such a serious conversation.

Especially since there wasn't much to discuss anyway because there was no way in hell I was keeping it. So me not telling him would actually be more out of protecting him and less about me continuing to keep things that would affect him a secret like I'd already promised not to do anymore.

It was the easiest and least confrontational route though so I didn't have to do much justifying to swerve into that lane as I remade the bed, freshened up then prepared for his arrival. All I had to do was play it cool and keep my lips zipped for the week he would be spending with me then I would be free to handle things on my own.

DANCE DANCE BABY DANCE

The only problem was that the second I heard the door opening my nerves finally got the best of me, my body spazzed the fuck out and I basically ruined everything. I had timed the sending of my medium ashy picture to right when he would be a few minutes away to prepare him for what was waiting, me bare and lazily draped in the white expensive sheets with just a classy touch of crack showing. The captioned frame around it asking him to come finish tucking me in was a last minute decision, but it had been a waste of time too since there was nothing remotely sexy about the scene he stepped into.

Picture it: France. Springtime. Me, melanin popping, back arched, naked and thicker than cold peanut butter waiting for my man just like he'd expected. Surely a sight to be seen, right? Except it was supposed to be on top of the nice hotel bed not holding onto the toilet and hurling out the guts he'd just planned on getting into.

I heard my baby instantly spring into action, dropping everything and running over to me then doing his best to hold back my hair. It had been too late for some of the shorter locs that

DANCE DANCE BABY DANCE

framed my face though and I didn't know what grossed me out more, having my hair dipped in toilet water or being covered in vomit until I realized that it didn't matter since both were happening at the same damn time.

"You good now?" he asked after carefully helping me to my feet then steadying me against the cool marble on the sink.

I quickly nodded before covering myself and stepping away from the open bathroom door. In his rush he'd left the room door ajar and with the way things were arranged anybody walking by a second ago could have seen all up and through my birth canal.

It took him no time to shut then lock the door, but by the time he came back to check on me he had already halfway stripped down to join me in the shower.

"My bad, choirboy, but this rendezvous is over before we could get it started," I joked weakly as I turned the hot water on full blast, assuring him I was okay to go at it alone since I wasn't about to run it lukewarm for his comfort. But despite pretending he was melting when the water touched him, he insisted on staying and helping me get myself together.

DANCE DANCE BABY DANCE

"It's cool. We both about to be ashy tonight though because I ain't putting on no more lotion after this," he said to lighten the mood as he helped me get my hair clean then began to gently wash my back.

Usually when we showered together it would be because we were either rushing and running late or trying to get a quickie in before we had somewhere to be, but this time was different. We took our time lathering then rinsing while he became Inspector Gadget trying to get to the bottom of what had gotten me sick. We'd both had food poisoning in Sweden at the start of the tour so his natural assumption made sense, but when he asked what I had eaten today I froze.

I'd done my best to keep the water out of my face, but my salty tears had other plans as they boogied down my body, letting on that something wasn't right. *Fuck.* There was no way these hormones were already fucking me up this early in the game.

"Temp, what's wrong?" he asked with concern as he instinctually attempted to dry my eyes only his wet hands were no help and instead added to it.

We had been finished washing the vomit out of my hair

and off my body so I turned to shut off the water while I lied and told him that I was just a little emotional because I had missed him so much.

I'd wanted to lean on him about all of this the same way I had done everything else that'd popped up over the past year because I needed him. I loved him. But avoiding potential conflict was yet another habit that I still couldn't shake from my first relationship even when I knew the consequences with Theo would never lead to the same terrible places.

Unfortunately for me though I had fallen for somebody that

didn't believe in letting shit fester. If there was a problem he wanted it addressed and figured out immediately.

From the wide mirror above the his and hers sink I watched him watch me wrap my hair up in a towel and I could see from his confused face that he was wondering what he had done wrong. That just about broke my heart into pieces and I knew I couldn't let him blame himself for something that neither one of us had any control over...or rather something that neither of us had seen coming because we'd definitely had control over the year full of wild, raw sex that had gotten us here.

"Please don't hate me after I say this, okay?" I asked for his reassurance, trying not to sound like I was begging even though that was exactly what I was doing as he towel dried my still dripping skin.

"I couldn't," he promised from behind me after sighing like it had come from his soul. "Not even if I wanted to."

SO YOU THINK YOU CAN DANCE
TEMPEST'S INTERLUDE

One shouldn't just hope to be treated well. One must insist on it - Abraham Verghese

One thing for certain, two things for sure if nobody else in this world loved me I knew Teenie loved me. And having her in a crowd cheering me on as a kid made me feel like I could do anything since a hypewoman like that only came

DANCE DANCE BABY DANCE

around once in a lifetime.

Look at her go!

Dance, baby, dance!

Now as for my parents...I mean I guess I knew that they loved me. Like of course they loved their only child and they did all the shit you were supposed to do for your kid, but I didn't know if they necessarily loved *me* because they seemed to strongly dislike all the little things that added up to me being Tempest, the biggest of course being my love of all things dance.

At best they treated it like it was just something to keep me busy and uninterested in boys and at worst like a nuisance whenever it was time to leave work early for a recital even though they were always planned months in advance. None of that had ever been any real concern of mine though because long before Meghan Trainor had made it a hit record, I'd always known that I felt better when I was dancing too.

For as long as I'd remembered I would mimic every move I saw on TV, genre be damned, until it looked like I'd invented it. Early on I picked up what most people got wrong about dancing was that they simply tried too hard to be good at it.

DANCE DANCE BABY DANCE

The biggest part of doing it and doing it well ultimately came down to listening to your rhythmic instincts because our bodies knew what they wanted to do so all we really had to do was relax and let it move like water. The confidence I felt when I was dancing eventually transferred to every other area of my life and long before I had ever been shopping for a training bra, I became the most dangerous thing on earth: a little Black girl who knew she was unfuckwithable.

Finally at about eight my parents stopped telling me to sit my Black behind down somewhere and did what every middle class couple did when their kid liked to dance: they put me in ballet. Because my daddy, being a proud and old school 'Bama boy, claimed if I was gonna be around here dancing, he at least wanted it to be "respectable". That and him giving me a light warning pop every time I even looked like I wanted to tootsie roll or any other dance that put the focus on my booty taught me that there was good and bad types of dancing.

I would be lying if I said I'd hated ballet at first because I didn't, but over time it became apparent that even though the class was a mixed bag racially, I was still the antithesis to everything a ballerina was supposed to be.

I was the blackest, the tallest, and I had just enough meat on my bones to feed a family, but right when I thought about finding something else to do after school Teenie showed up, crash landing in my life like Dorothy and Toto in *The Wiz*. And since I didn't have many memories of her before then, I couldn't have even begun to imagine just how much unfiltered joy she was about to bring with her.

Now if by chance you'd heard about my Granma Teenie before what all came with actually meeting the phenomenal woman in person you might have expected to see a sweet petite old lady with knitting needles and a bible by her side. But instead even in her deep seventies you would probably come face to tits with a big tall brickhouse baddie holding a bottle of Jack, a cigarette and a boa if you happened to catch her on a show night. But then again according to her every night was a show night and not even a bad hip and arthritis in both knees could fully stop her motion.

Just like me she never could sit still and travelled the world as a singer and shake dancer until she couldn't anymore. And that woman had to be at least part magician because I'd never seen somebody chain smoke cigarettes the way she did but never smell like smoke. She had the best stories too, but I learned to take them with a grain of salt after a while.

Back then I didn't think of myself as a gullible kid, but for years that old bitty really had me out here believing that they had based *The Color Purple*'s Shug Avery off her early years down in Alabama juke joints. I didn't hold the truth against her though since as I got older I realized she was *both* Shug and Sofia wrapped up in one.

TANZANIA GLOVER

Because while she would prefer to knock your socks off with her wild singing and dancing, in the blink of an eye she could knock your head off your shoulders if you didn't show her the respect she demanded. And with a mother that had been timid from birth and scared to blink too hard let alone fight, I liked that energy because until she had come to live with us in boring old Ladera Heights, I had never seen that kind of spunk in a woman.

In fact the only thing I'd ever seen my mama put her foot down about with my daddy was locing my hair because she was a nurse

DANCE DANCE BABY DANCE

and didn't have time to be
wrestling with my head every few
business days after I'd sweated
out a style. And even though I was
the only loc'd baby in my school
at first I welcomed the change
since I had long been branded
tenderheaded with a Scarlet T, but
I mean who wouldn't be with the
way folks impatiently and
seemingly purposely ripped
through hair that had even the
slightest hint of a kink?

The *ugly* or as I preferred to
call it the *beginning* stage of
starter locs kept me jealous of all
the long and loose haired
ballerinas for years, but only
when I learned to work with

instead of against what I had naturally did I learn how truly beautiful and versatile they could be. And it especially helped when my cute neighbor EJ from down the block had said they looked like cool little snakes and couldn't wait to show me Medusa when he learned about her in school.

Look like that boy took a liking to you and won't let go.

From day one Teenie **never** liked EJ and if it had been up to her I never would have gotten involved with him in the first place. When I was younger I assumed it was because his grandmother was the ringleader of the group of women that sat around gossiping about her after learning about her excentric not so distant past life.

She didn't let it bother her one bit though and insisted on giving them a show since they wouldn't be able to stop themselves from watching anyway. Any given Sunday she made it a point to be the baddest in the pews no matter how hard my daddy tried to cover her up for church.

I guess he had also wrongly assumed that Teenie retiring her show meant she was hanging up her dancing shoes and the over the top lifestyle as well, but he'd been mistaken in the worst way.

Because those that couldn't do anymore could always still teach and every now and then she would even take her talents to Vegas to make some real money and remind herself that she still had it.

Once she had convinced him to bring us all to see her on the strip and I guess with it being during the day time and of course her being much older he assumed that it would be more family-oriented. According to her it was, but a few minutes into her performance had him seeing himself out meanwhile not even a fire could have gotten my butt out of that seat.

DANCE DANCE BABY DANCE

I couldn't believe my eyes. There were far younger and more beautiful performers that went on before her, but apparently everybody knew Teenie **always** closed the show. I found out firsthand then that it was only because nobody was foolish enough to go on after her. Apparently some had already learned the hard way that they had to get their little shine on while they could then get gone.

Yeah calling her a tough act to follow was putting it lightly and her performance proved to be more than just something to watch during dinner at the casino. It was an experience. The music. The movements. She controlled the mood of the room. Whether she wanted a laugh or a lip bite out of the crowd, she could command it. She had a gift.

The next time I got her alone I asked her secret to making everybody keep their eyes on her when she didn't even move as much or as quickly as she claimed she used to. That was when she had taught me my most valued lesson not just as a performer but as a woman too.

With a coy wink she met me at my level then said, "You got to sell the sizzle, baby. Not the steak."

I didn't fully understand or

appreciate the words then, but as I grew it made sense. What some might have called old meat, those who knew better would call dry aged since it was capable of producing the most tender bites a mouth could experience.

It wasn't just about her body twisting, turning and gyrating every which way. It was how she looked at you. Making meaningful eye contact made each person in the crowd feel like she was putting on a show just for us. She made us all feel like we were lucky to be in there because she was royalty and if anything *we* needed to be putting on a show for *her*.

TANZANIA GLOVER

I didn't know what to say when she told me that I had that same flame in me too. She said rhythm and music flowed through our veins and that Mama and Daddy were trying to tame mine by putting me in lily white Ms. Goddard's ballet, but not even that would purge me. We were natural seductresses and there was no sense fighting it.

Just you wait. When you're ready you'll bring a man to his knees with just the twist of your hips.

After that everything made more sense. My daddy was scared of a woman that could sizzle and that's why he had chosen my

DANCE DANCE BABY DANCE

mama, a beautiful creature worth worshiping, but she was safe with not a pinch of danger or backbone in her DNA. So nobody was the least bit surprised at his disapproval as I matured and got into more sensual dancing like Teenie.

"Not only could we save a buck, but we could make a few putting her on the pole now if this is where she's headed," he had distastefully said to my mama one night while berating her about pushing me into nursing instead of dancing.

It hadn't been from her lack of trying though because when you're Black and your mama was a nurse she did whatever it took to make you a nurse too. I understood why. They made good money and there would always be a demand, but that life just wasn't in the cards for me. If I had to be on my feet all day anyway, better believe I would be dancing.

And if he was being honest deep down he knew the ballerina thing was never gonna work out anyway for all the same reasons as before plus my final growth spurt around fifteen made me too tall for all the good parts. Still I wasn't allowed to quit so I stuck with it and played the background, but my heart was firmly and securely with the kind of dancing that wasn't so hellbent on technique and making everybody fit a mold.

It had also been with the boy down the block once puberty finally set in, but me and EJ kept things as platonic as possible since I was always on lockdown. And like yeah we had snuck kisses over the years and he'd taken me to prom, but with my head in the books and my feet in class and rehearsals I didn't have time for much else.

It was too bad I hadn't kept it that way too. Because for years I'd fantasized about the day we could finally go off to college and be together, but as it turned out he could've only been the man of my dreams if he was named Freddy Krueger.

Before experiencing one for myself if anybody had asked me how a woman could end up in a relationship with a man who wasn't stingy with his hands, I would've said low self-esteem. But in my case it turned out to be more than that since I was well aware of how pretty and special I was. I knew I had inherited my granma's sizzling flame and most importantly I knew I could have had another man before the drop of a dime. But I didn't want another man. I wanted EJ. Always EJ.

DANCE DANCE BABY DANCE

Even when he started hanging out with the wrong people trying to get street credit at UCLA. And still when he dropped out to pursue his rap dreams. I thought I was being loyal by sticking with him and letting him sleep in my dorm since he didn't want to go back home with his grandmother and get a regular job.

A big chunk of that misguided mindset had stemmed from watching the dynamic of my parents' marriage and the type of relationship I had with them. Not being able to give input on my life and being one of those *seen but not heard* kids had practically primed me for abuse and being taken advantage of.

I'd learned early that talking too much got me in trouble and I was often accused of back talk when really I was just a curious kid with questions about the world. And by the time people expected me to talk more, I preferred communicating with my body since nobody ever misunderstood me then.

But being attractive and moving your body well was a lethal combination in a partner for an insecure man like EJ. He assumed I had to be lying about how many men I had been with before him and accused me of cheating every chance he got.

Of course it wasn't true. He had been my first and only everything and everything I knew I had learned from him, for him and most importantly *with him*. But I didn't know any better then. Hell I didn't even know what having boundaries meant in a relationship let alone actually having any of my own to enforce. And how would I when my mama didn't?

While I could never say that I had personally seen a bruise or heard her crying, the way my daddy talked to her alone sometimes should have been a crime. Just like EJ he liked the thought of having a beautiful, dynamic woman on his arm but simultaneously hated the reality of potentially losing her since he knew he wasn't good enough. And even if my daddy had been putting hands on her like I suspected he could have easily hidden behind his badge like so many others since the saying *firemen cheat, cops beat* hadn't come from nowhere.

EJ didn't need a shield though since by the time he started getting physical I was more than willing to cover for him. Home wasn't but a few minutes away from campus, but I rarely visited because I knew they

DANCE DANCE BABY DANCE

would be able to see the changes
on me especially Teenie.

It would be years before I
was called pretty for a big girl, but
I definitely started packing on the
pounds after starting college.
There were too many factors to
pinpoint just one, but the stress of
juggling classes, dance and EJ's
fragile ego had me eating up just
about everything in sight.

That plus being out on my
own for the first time in LA with
all the new food options that
home lacked was a recipe for
overindulgence. And since no
more ballet meant no more
restricting and obsessive calorie
counting I began to eat the

emotions I used to bury.

It wasn't all bad though because despite the unhealthy way I had gotten them, I instantly appreciated my new curves that had been pretty much nonexistent before. They added more oomph to my movements and for the first time I didn't look like a little girl pretending to be sexy. I *was* sexy.

EJ liked the new thickness too or at least he did at first until he saw the attention it brought. I was fresh meat on campus and had the nerve to be the fine, juicy kind too so of course I got approached everywhere we went. Although turning down the other men did nothing to ease his mind and instead it just made him lash out and keep me tucked away.

Looking back his jealousy had always been there lurking in the background though down to him not wanting me playing with other kids in the neighborhood. Because let him tell it everybody was jealous of me, him or us and it had to be us against the world. It took years before he had thrown the first punch, but he had been abusing me for years.

Nowadays I knew that if a man purposely hit or broke something I loved he just wasn't ready to do it to me yet, but as a dumb teenager when he was upset and breaking the secret stash of CDs that I kept at his house I thought he was just really, really mad that he couldn't see me more.

As time went on I stupidly romanticized the isolation and even let him convince me to move off campus into an apartment we couldn't afford because my roommate rightfully got sick of his constant presence. He'd actually started making some money and a name for himself in the city by then, but since he liked to stunt for the stunnas we never really could get ahead.

I knew I couldn't go to my parents for money without too

many questions being asked so naturally Teenie had been my first stop to get us out of binds. I didn't get too bad of a lecture though because she knew I was already familiar with one of her favorite sayings: "Purse first. Ass last." Still after a time or two too many of making her dig in her bra for rent money she gave me a refresher for the ride back to the city.

Every now and then a woman might let her guard down enough to let a man play with her heart, her pussy or both but never her pocketbook, you hear?

The financial abuse was actually the least of my worries

though because once he officially got me alone it became apparent that he would no longer control his hands either. Back then I blamed the escalation from just verbal abuse on the drugs he was doing even though I didn't know which one had done the most damage, the coke, regional fame or the insecurity. But it didn't matter because I saw with my own eyes just how dangerous the cocktail could be.

I distinctly remembered watching Ike and Tina as a kid and being so sure of what I would do if a boy ever tried to treat me like that, but my young mind had underestimated how physically intimidating and emotionally manipulative men could be. EJ would blow up then act like the perfect boyfriend for a few weeks until the next thing set him off so I walked around on eggshells trying to anticipate his mood and avoid his mantrums.

I still thought it was okay though because he was always so sorry after he sobered up and he always made it better. If he had punched a hole into the wall he would fix it. Slammed me into the same wall? I got a massage. But after a while there wasn't much he could do for the black eyes, bruises, busted lips and eventual broken bones.

TANZANIA GLOVER

I found excuses where there weren't any, attempting to justify the way he treated me. Because if even my favorite songs had highs and lows then of course a relationship would have them too, right? And he didn't have anybody besides me that he could really count on. And—and his parents were on drugs and had mental health issues and his grandmother's only solution was to pray about everything.

I stayed with him because on top of boiling frog syndrome and feeling obligated, I still wanted to believe the little boy who used to eat graham crackers with me on his back porch was still in there somewhere.

For seven years I pretended that we were still in love and not growing apart only he wasn't as good at pretending as I was and occasionally let his fists show how he really felt about me. Obviously I had gotten used to the chaos and the dysfunction had become my normal, but when my buzz became loud enough to drown his out was when the real terror took place.

I booked lots of jobs because I was out here dancing like the rent was due since it really was. And with music changing as quickly as it did his sound was fading faster than the few genuine good times we had over the years.

By the time I'd graduated he wasn't bringing in any money and no matter what I did to make him feel better bitterness and resentment had become mainstays in his life. Oh and coke too. He had become a full blown Powder Ranger so him and coke were like two peas in a pod. Let him tell it he was the furthest thing from an addict, but other than liking how it smelled there was no excuse for how often that booger sugar found its way under his nose.

For me though? My drug of choice had always been dancing and I truly believed that the happiness I got from it bothered him. Because even going through the worst of it all I still had something I cherished more than anything and nobody could ever take that away from me.

Dancing was about so much more than just moving my body. I had to give myself to people. Every tour, every city, demanded my best and if I didn't deliver I knew I probably wouldn't be asked back. If the rehearsal didn't look like the show then I needed to rehearse more. If the show didn't look as good as the rehearsal then I needed to rehearse more. In fact there really was no such thing as rehearsal because every time I hit the stage I had to give it my all.

And because of that, me loving and giving myself to something other than him, I believe he tried to take dancing away from me. He denied tampering with my birth control pills when I found the strength to confront him about it, but I guess it didn't matter either way because what was done was done. I was pregnant and faced with a decision: go on tour or abort because I couldn't do both.

When faced with a similar decision at a younger age than me, Teenie had chosen the show. I never asked if she had any

DANCE DANCE BABY DANCE

regrets, but I did know my daddy resented her like hell for keeping a packed suitcase and leaving him with her sister whenever she had gigs. My grandfather had been one of those men she warned me about, the ones who tried to put out a woman's flame, but she let him know early on that she would keep it lit with or without him by any means necessary. And she did.

I guess in EJ's eyes I must have spent too long contemplating because the fact that I didn't automatically choose **his** baby over my career made him fly into a rage. He beat and kicked me like he had never done before and by the time he was done he had made the decision for me. I would have neither.

Miscarriage was technically the right word to use for what'd happened to the baby, but the totality of the experience felt more like an attempt on our lives. And I must have looked even worse than I felt because he was scared to let me go to the hospital to get help for a couple days and tried his best to take care of me at home.

But when it was clear the first aid kit we had in the bathroom wouldn't be enough to patch me up this time he finally dropped me off at the ER. His tires screeching away was the last thing I heard before I remembered collapsing at the entrance.

When I came to again in a hospital bed I wasn't sure how much time had passed, but I knew it was a good amount when I saw how much hair had grown on my body. The mild hirsutism from my PCOS wasn't the worst part of the condition since I always stayed on top of it so nobody would even know I had it under normal circumstances. But the shame of now being *one of those women*, a victim, must have been too much for my mind to bear so it had decided to cover myself up and focus on the shame of having hair where I didn't want it to be.

But as it'd turned out I may have indeed been in similar company because when I was finally able to sit up and speak back the first thing my mama asked me was what I had done to make EJ so mad. Teenie, who had by then been dealing with early signs of dementia, still gave the only right answer to a ridiculous question like that.

Nothing.

Because there would never be an excuse to do what had been done to me or to take away what had been taken. If he had at least gotten me to the hospital sooner

DANCE DANCE BABY DANCE

my body's attempt to heal itself wouldn't have made the already bad situation worse. But the scarring and internal damage along with the hormonal complexities of PCOS had pretty much guaranteed a future successful pregnancy would be like winning the lottery for me.

And the irony of it all was if he had just given me more time to think I would have chosen him and the baby then tried to get back to business later. I would have figured it out because aside from time traveling to dance on prime seventies *Soul Train* literally all I had ever wanted was to be somebody's mama one day.

TANZANIA GLOVER

I'd been curious to see if my womb was capable of passing down that sizzling flame to a daughter since Teenie had first told me about it. And the thought of me never being able to have that was just plain old unfair. I was more angry about that than all that had led up to it because fucking up my past was one thing, but taking away possibilities in my future was unforgivable.

That was the moment I stopped mourning the life I'd been tired of living anyway. From that point on it was fuck EJ, his ugly ass grandmother, her dry wig and the generic graham crackers she always bought from Aldi. Teddy Grahams didn't even cost that much more and a bad ting like Teenie would never.

Recovery took a while. Learning to dance again was at the top of my list, but first the doctors just wanted to see me walk to make sure I had no significant lingering damage, at least of the physical variety because mentally I was still touch and go. But when I wasn't in physical therapy I just laid in bed all day feeling exactly like Ms. Etta since all I could do was cry too.

Eventually I could walk, skip, jump and use stairs on my own again, but it would still be a journey to get back to where I had been. And because of my fragile state nobody but Teenie would tell me anything about anything so I cherished those moments when I was left alone with her.

See Teenie had the tea and she spilled all that she could manage to remember in between telling me that I looked big for my age since sometimes she thought it was still the year she'd come to stay with us. Watching her have good days then was even harder than the bad ones though because they were just a reminder of how things should have been all the time. She couldn't even be left alone anymore and was the biggest reason my daddy had to finally retire from the force.

But back to the tea...so apparently my dad had gone looking for EJ all over the city but was only able to get in touch with his grandmother and the lies he'd told her were enough to make my head spin. He said the baby wasn't his. Said I had hit him first and he had the bruises to prove it. He was even thinking about pressing charges on *me* for all the abuse I had put *him* through for years. Jesus be a DARVO pamphlet...

Adding insult to injury, when I brought up eventually going to get my things with my dad I was told there was nothing to get. I still needed to see it with my own eyes though so after getting released with a mostly clean bill of health I went to see what was left of where I had once called home, but I swear it could only be described as the traphouse version of the last episode of *Fresh Prince*.

EJ had literally taken everything except the eviction notice on the door and even my car, the one thing he'd actually paid for, wasn't in its spot either. In an instant I was homeless, jobless and carless so I didn't bother checking our joint account since it had been overdraft even

DANCE DANCE BABY DANCE

before he'd taken off.

LAPD had come by the hospital more than a couple times as a courtesy to my dad, but I wasn't really interested in talking to them. I had my reasons other than being ashamed and blaming myself, but I knew they would never understand so I didn't even bother explaining.

I just told them I didn't know where he was hiding then turned over in my bed to look out the window and on the bright side. I had stayed too long with one foot out the door when I should have been down the block and around the corner, but at least now I knew better.

TANZANIA GLOVER

In that moment I was far from it, but eventually I would be okay. I would get back on my feet in every way possible then everything about the life I'd had with EJ wouldn't even matter anymore.

The most humbling experience of my entire life was moving back home into my old room. It was mostly the same, but with a few updates since Teenie's caretaker stayed in there some overnights while my mama worked.

It was very apparent that there was something fishy going on between her and my daddy, but I decided that it was none of my black ass business because I was only worried about myself now. If I had been there less than a day and picked up on it then surely my mama had too and just chose to ignore it.

The one thing I couldn't ignore though was her bringing her thirteen year old daughter over with her every day since she was out of school for Christmas break. Thanksgiving had come and gone with me lying in bed not eating much, but it still surprised me that Christmas was only a few days away since the magic I usually felt this time of year was nonexistent.

For the life of me I couldn't

remember if I'd ever learned that little girl's name, but her impressive taste in music came through the thin walls and introduced me to something that I had never heard before.

Only held you long enough to get one kiss
You had my nose and your mama's lips
You were handsome son, I don't mean to boast
But I think your heartbeat is what I'll miss the most

Ethereal was the only word I could use to describe the voice I heard that day even as it sang

DANCE DANCE BABY DANCE

about losing his newborn son at birth. And as sad as I was sure the experience had been I selfishly thought that he was at least able to see and hold his child to know that he was real. I hadn't even been pregnant long enough to know if I would be getting the baby girl I'd always dreamed of dancing with on top of being told I would probably never get the opportunity again.

This wasn't the pain Olympics though and truthfully I didn't know if I would still be alive if I'd gone to the hospital, given birth then come home empty handed. Having to clear out a nursery and return baby shower gifts alone would have had me out of my mind.

In my heart of hearts I knew bringing a baby into me and EJ's volatile situation would've been a mistake; still it was one I'd been on my way to make. But in the singer's case, being in a loving relationship and doing everything right and still getting the short end of the stick was cruel.

"What's the name of that song?" I asked as it faded out, clearly startling the girl as she sat alone in the family room.

I hadn't exactly been the most welcoming to her the last few days and only really peeked out of my bedroom to pee or grab a snack. I honestly still hadn't felt like being social with her or anybody else, but Shazam hadn't recognized the melody through the wall so I was forced to be nice.

"'Little One' by my future husband Theo Smith," she said excitedly as she held up her phone to show me his face on the case.

"Wait how old is he?" I asked confused because he looked way too young to be singing about such a heavy topic.

"Twenty-one, but he got a old soul like me," she said with a straight face like she didn't have even more milk on her tongue than he did.

"If you want I can play you something else. He grew up in church singing with his mama so us Angels be calling him choirboy, but he got some nasty songs too," she said in a lowered tone which made me smile a real smile and not just one to convince everybody that I was okay.

"Actually can I hear that last one again first?" I asked her as I fully emerged from my doorway to join her.

Timeless wasn't the word. The music she shared with me that afternoon was new and to my knowledge not sampled, but it still somehow sounded like it'd already been a part of my life before.

He also got major points for keeping the music misogyny free and family friendly, well for the most part because she definitely wasn't lying about a few songs really going there sexually. It was still done in a tasteful way though and before I'd known it I was on my way to being an overgrown Angel and listening to him every day.

I kept trying to put him in a box and figure out who he reminded me of or sounded like, but each new track I found led to a different sound and feeling. For me music and dance had always gone together real bad so not being able to move my body how I wanted to in my head was an adjustment.

I would be really feeling the beat and getting ready to jump up and hit it when I was reminded that I couldn't just yet because I still had more healing to do. Instead of getting sad though I just inhaled the upbeat tempos and hopeful lyrics then exhaled the bullshit. It helped too.

Because if I could have done anything other than two step I probably would have ended up just like the European peasants I'd heard about in an early dance class. There were lots of theories including demonic possession and poisonous food on why they suddenly and in mass decided to dance nonstop until they died, but it finally dawned on me that life had probably gotten so hopeless that their bodies did the only thing it could do to self soothe.

Since there was nothing left waiting for me in LA, when I was finally well enough to be up and at 'em again my parents finally got their lifelong wish for me. For the next year I remained under their roof, followed their rules and started school to become a registered nurse.

I'd gotten a quick cert to work as a CNA at the hospital

with my mama where the only dancing I did was with my patients to get them in a better mood. It worked most of the time too and not only made the day go by faster but also made me appreciate all the stories I got to hear about how the older ones used to get down in their youth.

When I was assigned to kid units it was always a bummer seeing them sick or hurt, but guess what managed to cheer us up ninety percent of the time? Promising to show them how to do a move before they were discharged or even having a celebratory dance battle when they felt better. It was too bad the good feelings didn't last longer for me though.

Filled with more ennui than I could handle, I did nothing but go to school, work then home, but in my free time I watched Theo from a distance and enjoyed his online content. I had never seen somebody who loved music more than myself until him and seeing him deal with the loss of a baby in real time was almost as therapeutic as the actual therapy I had started attending weekly.

Of course I didn't like knowing that somebody else had gone through something so painful, but at the same time it was comforting not feeling as alone and getting confirmation that there was still a lot of life left to be lived. But if I was keeping it all the way real, there was for sure some weird parasocial thing going on that I'd never really felt with a celebrity before. Like every other teenaged girl I had been a screaming *fan* of all the great boybands of the past, but this was different. I was becoming a whole damn air conditioner when it came to Theo Smith.

I wasn't that much older than him, but I still felt too grown to be smiling like I did every time he went live for his Theo Thursdays. It certainly didn't hurt that he was even cuter in motion, but I had fallen in love with his voice before even seeing his face. It was like I saw colors when he sang. His lyrics and melodies painted pictures for me and that falsetto gave me more goosebumps than R.L. Stine.

In the moment I didn't realize what it had actually been, but before long it dawned on me what he'd done for me. He had literally gotten me out of bed and given me the gift of having something to look forward to again. It'd been missing for so long too because I didn't give four-fifths of a fuck about clinicals or head-to-toe assessments. Like every other day of my life since I could remember, the only thing I couldn't wait to do again was dance.

And right when I was feeling antsy as hell and asking myself if I was really about to continue wasting everybody's time and money in school for a career and life I didn't want, an old friend hit me up out of the blue. Coincidentally or maybe not I'd been grinning watching Theo live when I got the call and contemplated if I should just return it when he was done, but something told me just this once choirboy could wait.

Ainsley and I went way back to the summer programs we had

DANCE DANCE BABY DANCE

both attended at the Alvin Ailey American Dance Company in New York and during college I'd religiously taken her classes at Seventy-Seven Studios. When I was at my brokest and truly couldn't afford the fee she would cover it, saying she just loved how her choreography looked coming from me.

She was only a few years my senior, but she had this life thing figured out and had worked her way all the way up to being the dance captain for thee Bianca King. For years I'd wondered when she would finally invite me to one of the private auditions since that camp didn't do cattle calls anymore, but every tour I was left disappointed and questioning if I would ever get a turn.

She made small talk for a few minutes then finally excitedly told me to come out from whatever rock I'd been hiding under lately because it was about time we made history and fucked up some stages as tourmates…after my audition of course.

I almost dropped the phone. No wait I did drop the phone then my excitement just as quickly as I'd gotten it. As I reached to pick it up I looked down at the scrubs I had forgotten to take off when I saw Theo getting on live and remembered that I wasn't a dancer anymore. Or at least I wouldn't be in time for an audition of that magnitude.

With Ainsley on mute I screamed an agonizing, frustrated howl from the depths of my soul, not caring who in the house heard me. I had stayed ready for years, both hungry and thirsty for this opportunity, and now that it had come knocking I was out of shape and still halfway out of my mind. Fucking EJ.

After unmuting I sighed then let her know that on top of not dancing professionally in over a year, I had also been going through some deep personal shit and picked up more than a few pounds since she'd last seen me. I would have loved to say that food had become the homie lover friend that helped me cope sometimes, but I'd actually just gotten myself into another emotionally abusive relationship with it.

She must've heard the long day shifts, depression and Dorito dust in my voice since she paused for a second like she couldn't just go on her merry way without giving me some sort of consolation prize since she had burst in like Ludacris and disturbed my peace.

DANCE DANCE BABY DANCE

Finally she asked if I felt up to at least filling in for her weekly classes while she was on the road. Before I could get an excuse out she offered to let me stay at her place in the valley to housesit her dog too. Foolishly feeling too proud all of a sudden I thanked her for the offer then let her know I still wouldn't be able to do it, but without hesitation she clocked where my head was at then swiftly knocked it off my shoulders.

Bitch this ain't no fucking charity. I just don't want these niggas breaking in my shit while I'm gone. Now bring your fine ass over here and get this gate code.

I smiled. She was right. It would be mutually beneficial and after a second of mulling it over I figured that reclaiming my place in the city could maybe be just what I needed to finally get back to being me. Because this playing nurse shit was certainly not it and it never would be.

I was in.

Though I didn't know how since I had never done original choreography before. I was just known as the girl that could get any routine after seeing it once. But for the first time I could stop wasting my gift since I'd always seen movements in 3D, the way our bones moved and the best ways to make the meat that covered those bones jiggle and sizzle best.

I immediately started plotting and got the idea to really take advantage of this smaller opportunity so that the next time Bianca King came knocking I would be ready. I would take notes from people like Theo and take social media seriously, creating a consistent presence and engaging with people online. I might've been out here just winging shit before, but now my fine fat ass would make sure it was all flats, fried hard with a side of ranch.

Unfortunately Teenie's

dementia had continued to worsen during the time I spent back home so she was nowhere near as sharp as she used to be, but the day I told her I was thinking about going back to the city to dance again, she was as clear as a whistle.

Good and you bet not come back, you hear?

Just as I'd expected my parents were extremely disappointed with my decision and were not shy about letting me know it. I swear you couldn't tell a nurse and a cop shit! Saving lives was literally in their job descriptions and a daily reality so to them dancing just seemed so…trivial in comparison. But little did they know I was planning to save just as many including my own by moving my feet.

I lived dancing. I had a dream and I wasn't going to let it die just because the baby had. Because in a twisted way it freed me from EJ forever since I never would have left without something so traumatic happening. In a twisted way it was actually the kindest thing he had ever done for me.

The line that sat between love and hate was a lot thicker than most folks would like to admit and I knew firsthand since I had loved a man who didn't deserve to breathe the same air as me. He even doubled down on it by showing no remorse and once he saw that nobody knew about what he'd done, he didn't waste any time putting in work to get even bigger down in Texas with his new crew.

I knew he had people there on his mother's side so no doubt that was probably where he'd been since being on the run. I couldn't blame them too much though because I was sure he had lied to them about everything too and even I had unintentionally helped him get away with it by not seriously pursuing charges when I had the chance. But if we kept it all the way real what would have really happened if I'd told on him?

If I was lucky he'd have gotten a slap on the wrist and me a few sympathy calls in private, but ultimately he would have been very publicly protected and sided with like I'd seen with so many abusive men in my lifetime. Hell my own mama's first reaction had put the blame on me so I didn't think I would fare too well with the rest of the world.

And while I knew evil thrived in silence so suffering in it wasn't the answer, what was the alternative? I knew how the game went. Aside from my family

I hadn't told a soul about his abuse, but I'd still already gotten enough stitches for ten snitches. But ultimately I knew there was a possibility that I would still want to work in the industry someday so it wasn't even a question of if I'd keep my lips zipped or not.

Before knowing better I used to unfairly judge survivors that "let" their abusers roam free hurting other people until I had kept living and realized why. Being revictimized, scrutinized and called a liar, clout chaser, etc. would've been traumatizing as fuck not to mention at the end of the day I didn't actually owe anybody anything. After what I had gone through protecting my peace was priority number one and I made no apologies for it.

And who knew? Maybe one day I would feel comfortable sharing, but it would have to be from a place of triumph or supporting other victims because I never wanted pity for myself.

One of my favorite rappers Megan Thee Stallion had been right when she spit that while bad bitches did indeed have bad days too, we didn't need pity. We just needed time to regroup so we could bounce back even badder.

What'd happened to me wasn't part of the plan, but it was still a part of the process. And I was determined to make lemonade out of this shit even though life hadn't even bothered supplying me with the lemons. But with just a little sugarwater and lime I had all I needed to get me going again so I hit the ground running and didn't dare look back.

I had missed the city so fucking much I could cry. The people, the culture, and yes the bomb ass food. I could have changed my name to New Edition right then because baby I was home again!

By the time Ainsley was done on tour, I was offered my own permanent teaching spot by the studio's owner so I had to find somewhere to live since Teenie's encouraging words had let me know that home was no longer an option. I ended up sharing a place with a few dancers from my classes and when I say my room was so small I had to go outside to change my mind, I was not exaggerating.

But I didn't complain because it was all mine and even though it wasn't my first time living in LA it was the first time I was living there free and there was no better feeling than that. There was even a tenant accessible rooftop that I would go up on some nights just to see the lights and think.

Thanks to the pollution I couldn't see much of them, but no amount of smog could keep the brightest stars from winking down at me and I liked that a lot. My life was nowhere near perfect in any kind of way and my relationship with food was still very complicated, but I used my time up there to remind myself that despite it all I was exactly where I was supposed to be.

I was still using Theo's songs as therapy then, but he wasn't the only singer whose music had touched me during that time period. Bianca King's younger sister Sloan was a supremely talented artist too and she had made an introspective song about trying everything to heal herself including attempting to dance away the pain.

It had been my jam and I'd done several different routines to it over the years, but it really hit different after what I'd been through the past couple years. Well that and as much as I hated to admit it, she was right and there was just some shit that couldn't be danced away.

Therapy taught me that pretending EJ's abuse and losing the baby didn't happen wasn't the answer because those experiences would always be stuck with me, but also just because they were there didn't mean I had to hold on so tightly either. The anger I felt, no matter how justified it was, was killing me and at a rate I didn't quite appreciate so I had to do something about it.

Instead of trying to get rid of it like the song had suggested, I decided to burn it and use it as fuel for my launchpad. And I especially loved the fact that I knew if EJ had been jealous of my ascension before, then he would be an envious wreck once I finally took off this time.

That was around the time I learned to leave all my problems at the dance studio doors and most importantly when I'd

DANCE DANCE BABY DANCE

learned how to shut up and dance.

DANCE MOMS

When you love somebody you can't just listen to 'em with your ears. Sometimes you gotta listen with your heart.

Granma, you got that from Pocahontas.

Chile hush. They got that from me. - Ruth "Teenie" Randall née Walker

Time usually didn't exist when I was alone with Theo. Sometimes I would look up to check it and hours would have flown by when it'd felt like just a few lazy minutes had passed between the two of us. But sitting there on that beautiful bed under the dim romantic lights talking about my past, I'd been more than aware of the second hand throwing that ass in a circle at least ten thousand times.

By the time we stopped to come up for air both of our skin was bone dry only ashyness was the least of our worries then. Tears had welled up in his eyes a few times as we drove down the bumpy road of memory lane, but they didn't outright spill over until he heard me use the A word.

It was finally his turn to talk, but I could tell from the lines in his forehead that all the built up emotions had weighed his tongue down something serious. I stayed quiet while he stared over out the lattice window, trying to be just as patient with him as he had been with me all night.

The light rain I'd gotten caught in earlier in the day had finally picked up into a heavy downpour. It always felt personal when raindrops hit windows like that since the slick and gloomy city streets were practically telling everybody to gon' head in for the evening.

DANCE DANCE BABY DANCE

I was more than exhausted from talking so I was thankful for a break from it and the bottle of water he'd gotten me to soothe my hoarse voice which had actually cracked a couple times from overuse. My locs had been thoroughly cleaned in the shower, but knowing where some had just been made the damp hair on my spine feel dirty all over again.

I really needed to blow dry them some before bed and I was getting awfully sleepy waiting, but I knew letting him get his feelings out too was more important so I just yawned a couple times until he found his words.

"So I understand why everything you've been through is making you want to do this, but I guess I'm still just confused why you're not happy when we literally talk about having kids all the time."

"Well yeah about maybe trying IVF or a surrogate in a few years. Not now in the middle of my dream world tour."

"I get that too, but truthfully unless something bad could happen to you I don't think that route should be an option for us."

"Well it is and I'm not about to go twelve rounds with you about it when I've already explained how and why I came to this decision."

"And it's just your decision?" he asked as if I hadn't deliberately presented it as a fait accompli.

"Until you get a pussy to push a baby out of? Yeah."

The second the words left my lips I knew they were harsher than they needed to be. He was taller than me by a lot but not by enough to not see eye to eye about something like this so before he could even react I decided not to fan the flames any further and leaned over to bring his face down to mine.

"I will listen to whatever it is you have to say, but at the end of the day it's up to me and I need you to acknowledge that before we go any further."

His stubborn side clearly wanted to reign supreme, but keeping our eyes synced then and preemptively waving my white flag with a soft kiss made him slowly agree with a nod.

"But Temp, what if this is our miracle baby? I know it's not like how we thought it would happen, but so what? What about this relationship has been? Because I wasn't planning on meeting you. I wasn't planning on falling in love with you. And I damn sure wasn't planning on needing you just to breathe like I do now," he said before letting out a big exhale from a breath he'd made himself hold.

"You're my good luck charm. Since before I even met you. It's going to work out for us. It has to. We both know I ain't shit, but you're too good of a person for it not to work out for us," he said trying to coax a smile out of me, but instead it just made me sigh because he wasn't making this any easier.

This was why telling him was both the right and wrong thing to do. I thought long on what to say next until I heard a voice several seas away speak to me.

Just 'cause a man want to make you a mama don't mean he want to be a daddy.

"Why do you even really want kids?" I asked thinking the Teenie inspired question would catch him off guard, but not more than a second or two passed before he responded.

"Because I've never wanted anything as bad as I want to be with you for the rest of my life and I want kids to be a part of that. Every day I prayed for this to happen, but I guess I ain't really consider that the timing of it all could make my blessing your curse."

"Okay let me rephrase it

then. Do you want to take care of a baby or do you want to watch me take care of a baby because those are not the same thing?"

"What is that supposed to mean? You think I wouldn't help you out?" he asked like it wasn't a well-known figgety fact that men wanted kids the way kids wanted pets; there for the fun shit and dassit.

"Not if you're already framing it like you would be doing me a favor. Because I wouldn't need 'help'. I would need a fully physically involved parent," I explained, but I could tell implying that he would be a hands off dad made him super-duper offended.

"Look I think you would probably mean well, but a man's definition of parenting is a lot different from a woman's definition. Just look at your family. Your daddy has always been there and he doesn't hesitate to set you straight when need be, but your *mama*? That lady still happily comes over to cook and do your laundry every week."

And by no means was I trying to throw that in his face because it really wasn't an issue. I loved how tight he was with his family and touring with DeeDee last year had made her a lifeline for me even after getting off the road. At first I'd been cautious about getting too involved with the Smiths, but it really did just happen naturally because they were all always around and worked like a team to make his life easier.

In fact that was why I had done us all the favor of not taking him too far away when finally choosing a new place to lay our heads. Of course his mama had still found fault in that too because she was his accountant and knew firsthand that life post Tempest looked a little different for him.

Before me Theo had been great with money, living in a

starter mancave-ish house and driving a luxury but still sensible car and now he was out here magic trickin' to the max with no end in sight. Because the Birkin, the Benz and my bills were one thing, but apparently she had finally tried to put her foot down about the warehouse he'd bought to convert to my dance studio.

In her defense though we *had* found it right in the middle of house hunting in the hills so it did look like he was doing a lot at once, but regardless she was a woman of a certain age so she should've known the game by then—there would always be a premium to pay for pussy...or at

DANCE DANCE BABY DANCE

least it should have been according to Teenie.

As a naïve teen I remembered discarding the advice, thinking the transactional dynamic she described was basically prostitution, but I kept living and learned that a truer truth had never been spoken.

Hoes don't leave no money on the table, baby, but any woman with sense know just 'cause it's for sale don't mean you let just anybody buy it.

The flipside of that was still making sure to always have your own too though because solely relying on a man's word or wallet was Tom Cruise level risky business. And as the saying went giving a man the power to feed you also gave him the power to starve you.

Experience had taught me to apply that same sentiment to outside validation too which was why I was no longer pressed about fitting into anybody's mold. I refused to worry about if I was too much or not enough for the rest of my life. After EJ I had decided to permanently be on my Goldilocks shit since I'd already been just right.

I did have a sneaking feeling that the optics of our relationship mattered more to Theo's mama than how much he was actually spending on me. She'd gotten used to the idea of sweet little Natalie being her daughter-in-law so it was more than obvious that her baby boy falling in love with somebody that could give the twerk team a hard day at work wasn't on her bingo card.

I understood it, but I would've driven myself crazy if I'd kept on caring about showing how multifaceted I was to the masses. I could twerk, tap then tango without missing a beat, but at the end of the day none of that mattered because I was whatever they wanted me to be. And yeah I could have put those feelings to the side and had a heart to heart with my man's mama, but I felt like she would have seen my character for herself if she just opened her eyes and looked beneath the surface.

As fine as I knew I was when I really put that shit on, my everyday clothes and Temu Tempest lifestyle was pretty much as basic as they came. I lived in sweats and spandex for comfort and movability and unless I was on stage "the glamorous life" had very little appeal to me. And sure I acted like a bird for shits and gigs on the 'gram and with my girls sometimes, but I had no feathers to ruffle or points to prove to anybody.

I didn't even flex or flaunt all the trick gifts I'd gotten from thirsty niggas over the years. At least ninety percent of it, including things I'd gotten from Theo, was stored and insured so that I could have something to sell one day if times ever got rough again.

Because simple I could do, but being broke didn't look good on nobody and I vowed never to be it again if I could help it especially while being with a man. Because poverty mixed with patriarchy would always be the most expensive pain in the world.

Until Theo I had been my

own village because my parents were getting older and while I had plenty of dance friends, there wasn't anybody that I would necessarily describe as close. So that meant that one wrong decision, like having a baby out of season for instance, could literally change everything for me.

Theo was more than aware of all that, but since he considered himself to be a standup guy and a certified lover boy he wasn't exactly interested in hearing me use that line of reasoning as an excuse.

"If there's one thing you don't have to worry about, Temp, it's what type of dad I'mma be. I

DANCE DANCE BABY DANCE

told you from the start when this time came that I had you, right? Well it's here and I got you," he promised sounding as smooth as Tennessee whiskey and as sweet as strawberry wine with a hand on my face. "I'll always have you."

"How are you gonna 'have' me and a baby when it's time for you to tour?" I asked trying to bring in some logistics before I started falling for what I was sure would be future song lyrics of his.

"I'll get a bigger bus and the baby can come with us."

"Okay but they don't stay babies for long. Kids need structure and stability and school to socialize."

"So then I'll only tour in the summers when it's time for school. What now?" he asked trying to be cute in my face since he thought he had tripped me up.

"You have an answer for everything now, but it's really not that simple."

"Yeah but it's not that hard either. We're not the first entertainers to raise kids so why don't you want to at least try this with me?" he asked like it wasn't obvious and actually waited for me to give him an answer.

"I don't know, maybe it's because I don't feel like being reminded about what my body may not be able to do!" I snapped then quickly reined it back in. "Theo, you're a man so you'll never get this part of it, but just take my word that it's really fucking hard."

"I know that and I wish there was a way for me to make it less hard for you, but just because it would be easier on me doesn't mean that it would be easy," he said defensively alluding to how devastated he'd been after losing the baby he'd shared with Natalie.

That sobering point made me want to stop pussyfooting around and let it all hang like my titties fresh from doing a day long bid in a bra. Because he really needed to see how life changing this situation could be for us both and not in the way he wanted it to be.

"Theo, this relationship works because we fuck a lot and don't have much to argue about. A baby changes that out the gate. You think you're ready because you can afford it, but that ain't got shit to do with sharing my time and body with somebody else. Actually forget sharing. The baby gets priority, but most of y'all don't understand that until it's too late and then boom it's over before we blow out the candles on the first birthday cake. I don't want that to be us."

"It won't be us because I'mma be right there in the sleep

deprived trenches with you. And you already know I ain't no jealous ass nigga," he claimed practically begging to be called out on his bullshit.

"Says the man that sideeyes me when I listen to other men's music for too long."

"Because why you be singing that shit so hard for?!" he answered predictably falling right into the trap I'd set for him.

"Luther though?!"

"Especially niggas like Luther!" he playfully shouted and I knew he was alluding to my gay dance partners on tour. "I see you and I know you be out here trying to turn them out too. Or would it be turning them back in?" he asked with a contemplative head tilt.

"Stop it before you get cancelled again," I said pouncing on him to cover his mouth as we fell back on the bed laughing.

For a minute we forgot all about the main topic at hand and landed right into a big pile of our usual banter. I didn't see it happening anytime soon, but I knew like all relationships that the passion would eventually fade someday. The laughter would always be my favorite part though and I hoped we could always make room for it. Because I knew what it was like to not have anything to smile about in a relationship and I also knew what it was like to have one beaten out of me.

That thought led me directly to another uncomfortable revelation. The last time I'd told a man I was pregnant I ended up in the ICU, but with Theo I had literally just been showered with love and understanding and then listened to for as long as I had felt like talking.

We definitely needed that breath of fresh air in the room to clear the tension and for a while after I laid there with my head on his chest thinking about all the other ways he was different than the men that'd come before him.

I remembered how embarrassed I'd been the first time I spent the weekend at his old house when I'd unexpectedly bled like a stuck pig all over him in our sleep. Like I literally had us waking up looking like Carrie at prom and the man didn't even flinch. And after forcing me to stop apologizing, he got some big ass diaper looking pads delivered with breakfast because he didn't want me to go home.

Teenie had always said you needed to see a man in all seasons and although the four we'd spent together so far were far from a lifetime, I'd seen how kind he was with everybody but especially with me. He was spoiled rotten, but it made him want to spoil the people he loved in return.

I hadn't had the best luck with vetting men before, but I was confident that I could cross without looking both ways first with Theo. He wasn't perfect and he definitely didn't always get it right, but the important thing was he never stopped trying to make it alright. And when I really thought about it...that was the exact kind of man you gave a baby.

Just don't never make more than you can care for by yourself or have a baby to keep a man. 'Cause a crying, colicky baby gon' make him leave 'fore it make him stay every day of the week.

Teenie's words rang clear and I knew that having a baby for a man was not it. That was why if I did have it, I would try to have it for me. Theo being a good partner and dad would just be the cherry on top because ultimately I wouldn't be able to live with myself knowing that I'd quit the one job I'd wanted the most before finding out if I was even hired in the first place.

I knew motherhood wasn't for every woman and as much as I wanted it, some days I did question if it was really for me.

DANCE DANCE BABY DANCE

But I was sure I had my answer when I realized that even if everything went wrong. If we broke up. If I had to do it all alone. If I had to stop dancing. I still wanted it. But the realization that simply wanting it real bad wouldn't guarantee us the happy ending we deserved still had my emotions all over the place.

I silently shed a few tears to myself on his chest, but it must have been just enough moisture to make him sit up to look down at me.

"Theo, you have the rest of your life to have an easy baby with somebody else," I began before he immediately cut me off.

"I don't want no easy baby with somebody else!" he said sounding frustrated at just the suggestion. "I want whatever comes with being with you or nothing," he claimed, but I wasn't sure either of us could take losing at the parental *Hunger Games* again.

The trauma my body had experienced was said to be too much to recover from and I'd accepted my fate ironically around the same time I'd learned of Theo's existence. Even with all the modern wonders of technology, Tempest maybe just wouldn't get the chance to be a mommy. And that was okay. I was still an amazing woman, daughter and dancer. And as much as I wanted to be a mother that would be enough for me. I just didn't know if in the long run it'd be enough for him too.

"But what if…what if I can't…I mean what if the baby doesn't…" I wrung my hands because just the thought of giving my all and trying but still losing broke my heart.

"Let's not even go there right now. I don't want to bring any negativity to this," he said trying to console me by pulling me into a hug, but I sprang up instead.

"No! The odds are not in our favor, okay? So unfortunately we do have to go there. What's gonna happen if we try and the baby doesn't make it?"

"That won't happen," he began then sighed after a pause, "But if it did then we would take a break from everything and deal with it together. We would go wherever you want to go and do whatever you want to do or nothing at all. We would talk and…just be until you felt like shutting up and dancing again."

By the time he finished his hypothetical scenario the tears in his eyes had respawned and spilled again as he nodded a hard yes to my question. "You promise?"

DANCE DANCE BABY DANCE

"I promise," he said with conviction before trying to quickly dry his eyes and tell a Black dad joke. "So am I buying the Burberry shirt or what, Temp?"

"I hope so, choirboy," I responded when I realized that I had lived my fears for way too long and it was about time to start trying to live my dreams.

I summoned him to come back up and lay with me. Both our towels had long loosened so he rested his head on my bare breasts then threw two out of his three legs over on top of mine. We were nuder than nude and holding onto each other tightly, but it wasn't the least bit sexual.

I loved times like these when he would give me kisses all over for no reason or just a simple, flirty smack on the butt to let me know he saw me. There weren't enough words to say how much I appreciated how our moments of intimacy didn't always have to lead to sex even though he was definitely always ready to go when I was.

For a minute there it was looking like we were in the clear and like we would end the emotional night on the same page and side of the bed. He was satisfied that I'd agreed that before we made any rash decisions that we would see a doctor to make sure it was a viable pregnancy.

But our next issue immediately surfaced when I brought up having to let Bianca know that I'd be leaving the tour soon either way. Because now that we'd jointly decided not to terminate, whether I stayed pregnant or not there was still no way I could continue on mentally no matter how much I'd convinced myself before.

"Wait no. You can't just quit dancing."

"I'm not quitting. If it's safe for me to do I would still teach my classes," I promised since there was no better feeling than making a dancer's leave out leave town after realizing it had no business coming in my class not tied down. "But you and I both know I cannot be pregnant on *this* tour especially," I said gently as I connected my forehead with his.

Bianca was the prototype for professionalism and aside from being off beat there was no greater dance sin than to drastically gain or lose weight on tour. The costumes were expensive enough on their own, but big alterations at this level could get costly and were sometimes impossible to do on short notice.

DANCE DANCE BABY DANCE

I didn't know how far along I was, but we had a little over six months left on the road and two before we even left overseas. I wasn't sure how long I could hide a bump for since even though my hip to waist ratio gave the illusion of a flat stomach that was far from the case.

"Maybe other people can't do it, but you're Tempest fucking Randall. You can do whatever you want to do and this is your shit they're out there dancing to so just talk to Bianca. She'll understand. She's a mama and she's done it before," he suggested before pointing out that one of the hardest parts for us, actually getting pregnant, was over and we would basically just cruise until the finish line if everything checked out.

I didn't agree. I mean yeah legally she would have to accommodate me, but it was such an unreasonable expectation for such a physically demanding job that I figured it wasn't even fair to ask in the first place. And of course it would have been amazing to stay on tour, have a safe pregnancy and somehow keep my dance rep intact, but literally nobody could have it all especially not at the same time.

Plus I really *really* **really** didn't want to rock the boat by

DANCE DANCE BABY DANCE

asking the universe for too much too soon...because a healthy baby would suffice for now and I would worry about shaking what my mama gave me later.

Theo, still on his campaign for me to finish the tour, brought up every performer he could think of that had done shows while they were expecting. My face remained stoic and unmoved though until he named Janet with a smirk which earned him a hard but playful mush to the side of his head.

He had finally crossed off the number one item on his bucket list when he met the icon at her latest tour and baby if Ms. Jackson had wanted him for herself that man wouldn't even have remembered my damn name. He had practically came in his seat just from watching her and that was the night I learned I was still just a puma in training since apparently she was the one and only head cougar in charge.

It was getting pretty late, but there was still no end to the conversation in sight since Theo was still insisting that Bianca would be okay with me remaining on the tour in any state since she was so happy with my work. And before seeing how her team operated for myself I might've thought the same, but

DANCE DANCE BABY DANCE

the well-oiled machine that surrounded her would never allow for any unpredictable variables which was how I had gotten the job in the first place.

Lately any knot in my stomach usually came from my morning til midnight sickness, but I could tell the queasiness I felt then was from the guilt that still lingered about me replacing Ainsley as dance captain. From day one folks whispered that I had shamelessly replaced the person that ushered me in, but I honestly hadn't even wanted to choreograph or be in charge of anything or anybody but myself.

I was just looking forward to

finally dancing with the both of them, but when Bianca King asks you to do something you do it. And she made it clear that she was trying to clean house when it was announced that nobody's spot was secure and every dancer would need to audition to be on the Revival tour with no exceptions.

Now Ainsley may have let her ego get in the way by outright refusing to do it, but I figured it was because she knew Bianca's team had just orchestrated the whole thing to push her out since the physical symptoms of her eating disorder had finally gotten harder to ignore. Since I'd known her she had always been a small girl, but the pressure to stay tiny as a dancer was intense and at a certain point it would undoubtedly get out of hand and this had been her point.

"Theo, you know nobody loves Bianca like I do, but asking Ainsley to audition was like spitting in her fucking face. She's given her whole life to this woman and she thought she was family, but she wasn't. It was just about what she could do for her. And it's business so it is what it is, but we literally give our lives to y'all and nobody ever really appreciates it. So now I'm thinking why was I just so ready to give up what could be my only chance at this to stand behind somebody else? Because it's always the show over everything and I stand on that. But what has the show ever really done for me besides given me a temporary high?"

I hadn't meant to raise my voice so much, but it was only because I sympathized with Ainsley on a deeper level since I had literally been in her shoes in more ways than one. I had also just witnessed her rehearsing until her feet bled for the Abu Dhabi concert we'd done together and at the end of it all it still wasn't enough.

DANCE DANCE BABY DANCE

And it had to hurt even more being replaced by a protégé and also somebody who was celebrated for dancing in a bigger body. Not for one second did the irony miss me and I made sure to be grateful I got the rare win since I was well aware that I was still the exception, not the rule.

"I think you're just saying all that because you're scared. And shit I am too. But I don't want us being scared to stop you from at least trying to finish what you started here," he reasoned, but I quickly waved him off because I was already clichéd out for the night.

"Nah hear me out for real.

This is supposed to be the top for y'all, right? Working with Bianca? But it's still just the beginning for you. You're gonna do it all because I'mma make sure you get to do it all. You're already a creative director in the making because your brain is in another dimension. You see the lights, music, costumes and movement as one thing but you don't half ass any of it. That shit is different, Temp. You about to take up a lot of space in this industry and I'm not just talking about all this ass I like feeling on," he emphasized by mannishly helping himself to a handful.

"I've seen it with my own

eyes. You stop the room when you walk in and everything moves around you. I'm never getting in the way of greatness like that. I'm trying to add to it in any way I can. And if this was something I thought you really didn't want, if your heart wasn't in it anymore then I would let you walk away with no problem. I wouldn't like it, but I would respect your decision. You want this though and it's already yours so I'm not letting you give up your dreams for me or anybody else, not even my big headed baby."

The size of Theo's head had never been any concern of mine since it fit perfectly between my thighs, but for the first time my eyes examined it before dropping to his broad shoulders and tiny waist then silently prayed that Jesus be a C-Section!

By the time he finished speaking my body was covered in the same kind of chills I had the first time I'd heard him sing. Teenie had always said that some men's only goal in life was to put out a woman's flame so hearing the one I loved promise to go out of his way to keep mine lit while staring in my eyes just did something to me. We'd been naked pretty much all night long, but right then and there he had intentionally chosen to bare it all

DANCE DANCE BABY DANCE

for me.

I knew what it was like to be in a crowd of thousands, to have everybody watching him while he was watching me. The fact that he had managed to recreate that same feeling a year later when we were alone made me wonder if he had loved me already back then...because at the moment it seemed like it was practically oozing from his pores.

All of a sudden I had no more tears left to cry so I did the only thing I could to show him how I felt. I put my lips on top of his to keep them silent then told him we would sleep on everything and finish talking in the morning. He nodded in agreement but clearly didn't pick up what I was putting down since he looked surprised when I let my kisses continue to drift down his body.

I was beyond tired and needed to lay my black ass down somewhere, but he had my ladybug jumping like a rope now and I knew I would sleep much deeper after a reset. Show day sex was always a big nono for me, but it was the least of my worries now because we needed this. I didn't want to think about no babies past or present for a while. *Fuck them kids* or better yet I wanted him to fuck me like he had done the last time I'd seen him.

DANCE DANCE BABY DANCE

"This what you call sleeping on it, huh?" he asked looking down at me with a cute smile as he bit his bottom lip.

"Yeah I haven't seen you in two weeks and for the first time all day my stomach isn't doing backflips so now I can do some on you."

"See that's how we got here now."

And he wasn't wrong. It certainly took two to tango, but I was the one addicted to the feeling of him swelling then trembling from inside out of me and that sweet agonizing look on his face when he felt my warm walls closing in on him. The second I even sensed he was close my legs would be locked and keeping him right where I wanted him.

Before I could comfortably get on my knees and take him in my mouth, he'd reached over for my phone to pick a playlist. I'd gotten so used to fucking him to music while we were on tour last year, but after getting home he wanted complete silence, telling me that all he wanted to hear was me since he couldn't turn my moans down like a song.

After a while even I had to admit that our mattress melodies, the groans and our bodies' rhythmic slapping, was music to

DANCE DANCE BABY DANCE

my ears too, but tonight I wanted a real soundtrack made up of his songs only. We had an endless amount of sex playlists, but he knew that one always made me go a little bit harder.

I couldn't really explain why either, but everything just seemed to hit differently when I was fully immersed in him, mentally and physically. It felt like he was touching every inch of my body all at once and I swore only Vishnu's wives could know my pleasure.

With a raised eyebrow he asked if he'd chosen the right song to start with and since I was already giving him a sloppy

French kiss below the waist I decided to answer in the romantic language too.

"Oui oui Monsieur."

"M-monster?" he moaned out which made me stop what I was doing altogether to laugh at his penile delusions.

"Why you always gotta get ahead of yourself?" I teased knowing good and well that thang really packed a punch.

Because honestly if it wasn't for his generosity and how much he loved me then it would have certainly been my favorite thing about him. Just thinking about how good he was to me made me run my tongue from root to tip before greedily slurping him up entirely again.

I loved that I was free to be myself with him sexually without being judged and I could tell he felt safe and trusted me with his body in return because he was always open to exploring and trying new things with me. I never could understand how other men loved and hated freak bitches at the same time, but luckily for me I did not have that problem out of Theo.

Our first time had been a night to remember, just pure lust and tension bursting at the seams, but it had gotten even better over time. He'd started off giving me his best moves, strategically using every part of his body to please me, but the real voyage to Atlantis happened when he learned what my moves were.

He became an expert at anticipating what I would do next and used the body language we'd developed to do what felt best at just the right times. I prided myself on my stamina since not many could keep up with me for too long and I didn't help matters by doing shit that I knew would make him tap out sooner, but a selfish lover he was not so he never let me get up unsatisfied.

That along with feeling the

intention in his strokes was new to me and something I really appreciated. Every time, every position felt like the man was literally trying to fuck his love into me and I had no choice but to lay there and receive it.

I didn't know what it was about being in the EU with me, but it had put him in a facesitting mood the last time he'd visited too so I wasn't that surprised when he suddenly offered me a seat on his mouth. Not wanting to be impolite to my guest, I got up to carefully climb up his body on the bed where he was already licking his lips in anticipation.

I knew he must've been

hungry since just like me he didn't eat much on flights due to his nerves, but I was not prepared for the amount of suction he used to draw me into his waiting mouth. I'd barely been hovering above him for a second when he locked my legs in place with his strong arms, knowing I needed to be buckled up for the ride he'd planned for me.

I used the headboard for support as I slowly wined against him how he liked, being careful not to place more on him than he could bear since he didn't know his limits sometimes. He would eat himself right into a coma if I let him, but I refused to let choirboy go out like that.

"Take your time," I teased as I eased up some so he could come up for air. "She's not going anywhere."

While catching his breath I leaned back on the two fingers he'd added to the equation from behind and complimented him for mastering that lost art too since I'd heard it was rare in his generation.

"We're in the same damn generation," he chuckled out. "You're barely thirt--"

"Aht. Aht. Do not say my fucking age out loud!" I threatened like we weren't alone because he knew the opps were always listening.

I wasn't insecure about my age, far from it actually because I was getting even finer with time. The industry was just disgustingly ageist so even though I was obviously older than him, I would still be "late twenties" until I couldn't pass anymore.

Before he could comeback I dropped it like it was hot on his chin then grinded my pussy on his face like my life depended on it. His body going stiff told me he loved that shit, but a minute later I got crystal clear confirmation when I felt a series of warm, wet ropes hitting my butt and lower back. *Look ma, no hands!*

Knowing the effect I had on him always kicked shit up a notch for me so it wasn't long until I was panting and shaking a tailfeather my damn self. I was suddenly aware of the music playing again when he told me to turn over, but I could do no such a thing since he had sucked out all the strength I had left. He had no complaints though and just took the time to kiss my thighs until I was ready to move again.

Now as much as I felt like just lying there and taking whatever he wanted to give me, my descent down his body lined us up perfectly and I instinctually kept pushing down on the familiar invasion. Still sensitive from his hands free nut, he hissed and grabbed hold of my waist as he begged me to turn over. I couldn't help but laugh at how dramatic he was being as I deviously ground into him.

"Why do you love that position so damn much?" I asked since I preferred watching him enjoy himself him on top with my ankles kissing his ears as he scratched an itch that only he could get to.

"Because…your backshots take me out too quick. Cowgirl, you're in control, winin with your titties all in my face. You know I can't handle this shit for too long," he said candidly before pausing to enjoy said titties all in his face for a second.

"Then with missionary, kissing and watching you say nasty shit. Forgetaboutit. The side is the only place I can really get my shit off and that's only if I don't look down at it too much."

"Is this you finally admitting that you can't hang with me?" I taunted until he pushed all the way in causing my mouth to fly open in a mix of a yelp and a moan.

"See. A nigga like me can hang anywhere. Now turn that ass over," he demanded with a smack on my butt to let me know he meant business.

The only place I let him boss me around was in bed so he took full advantage and talked his shit in here because he knew it just got me wetter. I brought my hips to a halt to do exactly as I was told since in this case turning the other cheek would still lead me to getting mine regardless.

With one of his arms supporting my head and the other holding up my leg, he clung to me closer as he pushed back into me. I had never met a man that could fuck half hard like he could, but just trust when I said that I was never coming up off him I meant that shit.

And that was why he didn't trip off my little dick jokes since he knew it was just an act to keep him humble. The second he was erect that dick transformed into a dique and left me looking as surprised as Pikachu.

With his mouth right above my ear, he decided to stop playing fair, talking me through it by singing along with the background music. I was here for every syllable of my private concert though and I didn't fold like he wanted until he put my leg down so that he could reach over and play with my clit.

Obviously there was nothing

dry about that area, but the way he started rubbing it was enough to set us both on fire. It was like he was suddenly on a damn clit conquering crusade and he wouldn't stop even after I had already crumbled to pieces in his arms. *Go DJ. That's my DJ.*

"Theo please!"

"Theo. Please. What?" he asked punctuating each word with a deep, mind-scrambling stroke. "Come for me, Temp," he begged then apparently decided that he was Craig Mack as he put a little extra flavor in my ear with, "Come again for **Daddy**."

Okay so peep this. I had a daddy that was alive, well and

DANCE DANCE BABY DANCE

ain't shit so I'd always thought calling a man that was gross and borderline incestuous. But coming from *my* soon to be baby daddy? It cleared the fucking room and in record time he replaced the tears falling from my eyes with the ones coming down my legs. I came so hard the room was spinning, but the high didn't end there as I finally realized that I was really about to try to make choirboy a daddy.

Without skipping a beat or letting me fully recover, he turned me over again so that I was lying on my stomach. I felt his stiffness returning with a vengeance as he kissed down my spine and demanded to be let back in only I had clamped my legs together.

"Oh my God. What has gotten into you?" I laughed out while still trying to regulate my breathing. Not wanting to admit complete defeat at being outstamina'd, I ordered him to go eat something other than me to give me a break for a minute.

"We done?" he asked smugly even though his breaths sounded just as labored as mine, but since he was still ready to put in more work I just let him have it and tapped the bed.

It wasn't up for debate. Late night room service always tasted

DANCE DANCE BABY DANCE

the best, but it went even harder then because it wasn't my food that I was fucking up. When Theo had put in his order for steak, fries and a salad I got more crackers and club soda, but the sight of his meal combined with him just trying to put me through the mattress had apparently worked up my appetite. He never minded sharing with me anyway, but he happily fed me until I couldn't eat another bite after learning that my stomach had been on E for days.

I didn't remember hearing him order any beignets, but baby was I glad they had sent them up since the one I had tasted like

TANZANIA GLOVER

Princess Tiana and nem were down there making them for us. Theo's sweet tooth was more than happy to fill up on them too since I'd eaten most of his steak, but he complained when he realized how much powdered sugar he'd gotten everywhere. I didn't mind as I just kissed some off his face and noted that eating them in our white robes had actually been next level genius.

Four empty plates and two full stomachs later set the scene for him to kick off round two on the couch, but my body decided that I'd had enough Big Fun In Baltimore™ for one night when it sent me flying back over to the toilet. Right on my heels and better prepared this time, Theo held my hair back like a pro and soothingly rubbed my back until the heaving and retching stopped.

I was too weak to stand so I just slunk down on the floor with my back against the sink as he got a couple cool towels to wipe my face and place against my hot skin.

"Will you marry me?" he blurted out before I'd realized he had one knee down on the marble tile in front of me.

"Ask me again later. I'm still queasy and you're covered in powdered sugar and pussy juice," I joked trying to buy some time, but he wasn't having any of it.

"So what?" he asked with a grin as he took a seat next to me. "I don't know about you, but to me that still kinda sounds like the best night of my life so what do you say?"

"I say…'Weren't we supposed to be waiting until the morning to finish talking about everything?'"

"Yeah that was the plan before, but I guess all that sugar from you and dessert woke me up so we're here now."

"Well then I guess since we're here you should know that we don't have to do this right now," I assured him as I reached over to put a hand on his face. "You're completely obsessed with me so I know marriage ain't that far off anyway. We can revisit this topic when the time is right, okay?" He nodded along in understanding, but his words didn't match the motion.

"Temp, I've been waiting for the right time since our first date. It was too soon then. Then it was well I can't do it after the tour because it would've looked like it was because I fucked up. Now you're probably gonna think it's because of the baby, right? But fuck all that. I want to marry you because *I want to marry you*."

He suddenly jumped up and

went to the bedroom. I thought about going after him to see what he was up to, but by the time I convinced myself to get up he was back and plopping down beside me again.

"I made sure I could be here for the first show in France for a reason. I was gonna do this in front of the Eiffel Tower after the show, but now you gotta say yes since you got me in my feelings and made me ruin the surprise," he said playfully as he pulled out a ring box.

"Not you were gonna give me a basic bitch proposal."

"Damn right I was and your basic ass was gonna love that

shit," he said confidently clocking my tea as he slid the pretty, sparkly rock on my finger. Somewhere his mama was crunching numbers and ready to pull out her hair, but he didn't let me think about that for too long.

"I know you've been complaining about not seeing it lit up so I was even trying to see if I could pay to get it done, but they told me I was in luck because they would be lighting it all night for Bianca anyway."

"Wait so first I was getting leftover, hand-me-down Eiffel Tower lights and now Plan B is proposing to me with my booty cheeks out?" I exaggerated making us both hold our sides with laughter.

"Look in my defense, your cheeks are pretty much always out so…" he said earning another muff to the face, but that still didn't stop him from smiling because it was done with the hand wearing his ring.

It dropped for a second when he saw me taking the ring off to put it back in the box, but before he got the wrong idea I let him know where my head was at.

"Next time you ask don't do it in a bathroom. No bedroom either," I instructed so there would be no room for error. "Or I guess it could be in the bedroom just not when we're naked, sweaty and wearing more powder than Scarface. Like remember when we were cuddling and watching Netflix in Sweden that night? That would have been the perfect time."

"So not after making love, but yes when we got food poisoning and we're watching a serial killer doc? Got it."

"Shut up. It's not about what we're watching or doing. It's just…Theo, that's what our lives will be like when we're not on stage or being who we are if the baby thing doesn't happen for us so it has to be enough. If you're okay with that then I can say yes."

TANZANIA GLOVER

"Tempest, in a bathroom, in front of the Eiffel Tower, literally anywhere," he began sounding like a Black Sam-I-Am as he took my hand in his, "My answer to you will always be yes," he said with conviction and showed that he meant it by kissing me even with my vomit breath.

After getting cleaned up for the second time, he sent me back to bed first, claiming he had an idea for a song that he wanted to record before he forgot it. I closed the bathroom door behind me to give him the illusion of privacy, but my ear was still firmly pressed to the door as I listened to him hum out a melody then

DANCE DANCE BABY DANCE

spitball lyrics until he found some he liked.

Out in Par-ie, we jamming
She's on another planet
Black card, she doing damage
But I just charge it to the game
'cause
She badder than Penny, Justice and
Janet

When I heard him wrapping up and preparing to come to bed I scurried over to pretend like I had been there the whole time. He was none the wiser as he shut the lights off then joined me from behind to hold me.

I had never been much of a

cuddler, but Theo was so affectionate it was like he wanted to live inside my skin sometimes. And no matter how long we held onto each other or how sleepy he was he still only ever let go after I did. I let him kiss the back of my neck and earlobes as I finally drifted off into the night praying that it really was possible for us to have it all.

I'd thought about Teenie all night long so I wasn't too surprised that I'd dreamt of her too when I got up to pee after a few hours. For a while I sat on the toilet as naked as the day I was born thinking about all that I had to do later on that day and how I would really be performing in Paris like the greats that had come before me.

To keep my excitement contained and allow me to fall back to sleep, I tried my best to get back to dreamland. I couldn't remember all the details, but the image of me standing alone on a stage with a big protruding belly was hard to forget even moreso than Teenie occupying the only seat in the crowd as she clapped up a storm and yelled for me to...

Dance, baby, dance!

TANZANIA GLOVER

BORN TO DANCE
THEO'S OUTRO

I finally found my rhythm when I realized that even the steps backward were part of the dance. - Melody Godfred

The scent of pineapples and oranges was already in the air when I opened my eyes so I knew Tempest had gotten in the shower without me. Her biggest worry lately had been giving birth *looking like a werewolf*

DANCE DANCE BABY DANCE

so I'd been on shave duty every time she started to get even a little bit of stubble. I wasn't complaining though because after getting her right, I could always count on a few wet kisses to get me right too.

For months I'd asked her if she needed my help reaching anything in there, but she always said she could handle it until one day she humbly woke me up claiming that she couldn't see it anymore.

"You can't see what?"

*"**It**. It's like trying to shave with a basketball in my lap,"* she'd complained, but personally I thought it was cute as hell when

her belly got so big that it had started to reach me before the rest of her could.

I considered myself to be an observant man, but even I had never noticed her having any more or less body hair than the average woman. After getting pregnant though her PCOS made hers grow even faster and since she couldn't do maintenance laser treatments because of the risks it posed, I finally learned another one of Tempest's *deepest, darkest secrets*—she had the nerve to be a human being that grew hair on her body just like everybody else.

Obviously there was more to it than that, but I didn't really see what the big deal was and thought it was just one more thing we had in common since I wasn't exactly hairless either. I mused that between the two of us we might've even had a baby yeti baking up in there since me and DeeDee both had a unibrow that rivaled Helga G. Pataki if we didn't keep it in check.

The sound of the water shutting off made me hustle over to the bathroom to pee where I found her about to brush her teeth. Her back was to me and the little ass towel she was wearing didn't leave a lot to the imagination so I startled her when I smacked her butt for the culture.

Everybody had been trying to guess if we were having a girl or a boy by how she was carrying, meanwhile I just wondered if she was pregnant in that ass too since it had been sitting up like a bunk bed I wanted to climb. At first she had wanted to keep the sex of the baby a secret, but sharing a stage with an international superstar a couple times per week kinda made it impossible.

Our announcement just said that everybody had been right since just when we thought we were getting Uno, fate had decided to hit us with a Draw Two card for one of each. I could tell that first doctor's appointment when two heartbeats were heard that Tempest wanted to worry twice as much, but I wouldn't let her. I reminded her that *if* something were to go wrong then we would act on it, but until then we would just keep taking it one day at a time. And it worked.

We made it all summer and halfway through fall on tour with no complications in sight, but the doctor that traveled with us agreed with her home OBGYN that inducing at thirty-seven weeks would be best for Tempest and the babies. The last show in Vegas was just a couple days shy of that so we had tried to cram in as much as we could before then.

A baby shower on the road just didn't make much sense so DeeDee had tentatively put together something called a Sip and See at the house for when we got back and the babies were born, but we managed the wedding planning all by ourselves.

It was non-traditional even by Vegas standards since we weren't drunk and stumbling in a chapel at midnight, but the simplicity matched the energy of the way she'd wanted me to propose to her. Her finger was way too swollen to accept the ring by then so she wore it on a necklace, but the important thing was that she had finally accepted my offer of forever after a boring, cozy night in bed watching our shows.

I was already talking about a big blowout anniversary party though because despite saying she was good with everything under the circumstances I knew a quickie wedding wasn't what she had dreamed of. And as for me, I definitely wasn't passing up any opportunity to show off my beautiful bride.

"You back to being Ms. Independent already?" I asked as I nibbled on her neck to get the fruity scent I loved straight from the source. She nodded her head then took a break from brushing to spit and tease me.

"I think I had enough of your assistance last night," she said because helping her out of her dress and into her pajamas had turned into me getting luckier than anybody else on the strip. I had no regrets though since she would be out of commission soon so I was trying to eat her off the bone every chance I got.

"I don't remember hearing any complaints, but then again your thighs were covering my ears so I probably missed them, huh?"

I caught the middle finger

she had stuck up in the mirror, but she lowered it just in time to stop me from taking off her towel, claiming we had to leave for the show soon. I knew she meant it when she even dismissed me offering up one more push present to add to her collection.

"No, Trick Jagger. It's the last day and I really don't want to be late."

"Ay that's Trick Daddy to you," I corrected before letting her get back to her routine, but I couldn't help but notice her wincing and holding onto the sink while I peed.

"You okay?"

"Yeah. It's just a little

pressure. The babies must've heard your voice and got riled up," she said making me smile about the connection I'd already built with them just from talking and singing to her stomach all the time. Literally the one checkup I hadn't been in town for still ended up with me talking on FaceTime just to get them to shift around how the doctor needed them to.

We were right down the street from the stadium, but Tempest insisted on rushing and making us wait until we got there to grab a bite to eat. I didn't question her reasoning or say anything when she stopped to catch her breath a couple times while she was getting ready, but right before leaving out I realized exactly what was going on.

The wet spot I'd woken up in wasn't from the fun we had the night before. Her water had broken.

"Are you in labor?" I asked as straightforward as possible and knew she definitely was when she tried to be sly.

"Define labor."

"Temp, what the fuck?! We gotta get to the hospital."

"But do we really though?" she asked nonchalantly while I unlocked my phone to text everybody the news. "I mean the show is only a few hours long and my mama was literally in labor with me for almost two days so I know I'll be good."

"Wait I know you're not thinking about getting on stage like this?" I asked with wide eyes surprised that she was surprised that I was surprised.

"Well you were the one who said I should finish what I started, right?" she said laying it on almost as thick as she was. "Baby, I'm too close to the finish line not to cross it. I promise I can do this," she assured me and I sighed because the look in her eyes really had me contemplating letting her do it.

DANCE DANCE BABY DANCE

"How far apart are your contractions?"

"At least twenty minutes, I swear. We've got plenty of time," she said convincingly until another one snuck up on her and caused her to hold onto her back in pain.

Half of me wanted to panic, but the other half sat everything down then grabbed both her hands and prepared for the incoming squeezing.

"It's okay. Just breathe and do like we practiced. Give the pain to me. I can take it."

Head to head we took deep, slow breaths together for about a minute until it went away and she was back to acting like superwoman again. I knew from reading that those were the quick, mild ones though and what she had in store when the contractions got closer together would last longer and hurt more.

I tried like hell to talk some sense into her, but she was determined not to listen so I got exactly nowhere. Luckily Dr. Kerry was right down the hall from us so before I agreed to anything we decided to get her opinion first.

To my surprise and dismay, after checking Tempest's vitals, dilation and the babies' heartrates with a doppler she said that while continuing with the show was unorthodox, it shouldn't have been a problem since we would probably just be walking around in the hospital until they were ready anyway.

For a minute I questioned her expertise since she had especially been loving the hell out of her job the last few shows, but when I saw for myself that all three of my babies were good I decided to let the biggest one have one last hurrah before making us parents.

When we had gotten back stateside, we traveled almost exclusively by my tour bus because the doctors didn't want Tempest flying any more than she had to. We had a local sprinter for the weekend, but the baby bag we needed was still on the bus so I sent DeeDee to get it to meet us at the hospital after the show then we finally headed to the stadium.

The contraction she had on the ride over nearly convinced me to turn around and go the other direction to the emergency room, but in between hee-hee-hooing she begged me not to. I had faith, but I had never been so scared in my life. The grip I had on the steering wheel temporarily made me lose all the color in my knuckles, but by the time I helped her into a wheelchair backstage they were back to normal.

DANCE DANCE BABY DANCE

Nobody suspected a thing since all tour long I had been there making sure she got all the rest she needed before each show. The rule was if she wasn't on stage or changing to go on stage then she had to be seated with her feet propped up.

It was a high stress environment for her, but when you really broke it down and accounted for the intermission, outfit changes and non-dance ballads Tempest really only performed for about fifty-six minutes of the almost three hour show and only two to three times per week. Outside of travelling it was actually less work than teaching her classes so getting medically cleared wasn't the issue she assumed it would be.

And just like I'd said Bianca ended up being one of Tempest's biggest cheerleaders and loved the response she got night after night from the crowds. Her show time had gotten reduced the last few weeks, but she was still moving well and doing shit pregnant and in heels that a grown man couldn't do in Timbs.

Back when I first found out she was expecting, I instantly dropped everything and built a team around her to make sure she had every comfort imaginable available to make up for how hard

DANCE DANCE BABY DANCE

she was working every day. And after getting a mild case of food poisoning at the beginning of the tour I had even appointed myself her food taster, but she claimed I had just found a clever way of getting my dad tax in early.

It made me proud when she told me that she had never felt more secure and supported before, but it did come with a cost. Being all hands on deck for her meant nothing new could be booked for me and little shit like appearances were either canceled or postponed. In some areas that ended up not being as simple as turning the hands on the clock to be on her time, but I made it work because real love was about sacrifice, not just how she made me feel.

Physically and emotionally being there for her was more important than anything and I figured if she could sacrifice her body, her career and potentially her life to bring our babies in the world then the least I could do was miss a few shows.

Jonathan will literally kill me if you cancel anything else for me.

My manager was well known for being all about business, but above that even he knew how much Tempest meant to me and that family came first. We had been putting in work for years,

DANCE DANCE BABY DANCE

but by mainstream standards I was still a new artist who needed to be doubling down on my efforts not slowing down already to have kids.

Because of that we had to get creative and work smarter not harder. My publicist Josie took on Tempest as a client and worked her little bony white ass off to keep positive planted stories about us in the news cycle and J had called in every favor tied to his name to land me a lead soundtrack song for two different but beloved film franchises.

One was for a kids' movie coming out around Christmas and the other was a fast car franchise on its last leg, but early reviews for my song had practically breathed new life into it. I swore that it was nothing but God looking out for us, but even if things hadn't fallen into place and gone in our favor I still would have made the exact same decisions.

I loved my fans and what I did more than I could put into words, but being behind the scenes and underground for so long I had gotten used to the idea of never really breaking out. If everything I had was gone tomorrow I knew I would still have dancing ass Tempest by my side so if being with her and having our babies was something I might regret one day, then I would just have to regret it because how could I not be with her and have our babies?

I love everything about you, Temp, even your smart ass mouth when you get mad. I ain't tryna change shit but your last name.

Tempest Randall-Smith in front of a wind machine was a sight to see. Literally any stage she was on would always be worth the price of admission, but seeing her kill stadiums her first time out and in her state sent my amazement through the roof.

I knew there were hundreds of people who put hard work,

sweat and tears into making the tour perfect, but nobody could convince me that it wasn't all her. I lost count of how many times I saw the show, but I never once got tired of it because it evolved over time, getting better and growing just like the belly she sported effortlessly.

Watching her show after show, somehow getting stronger and softer at the same time motivated the hell out of me and every time the light hit her it was something like magic, but never moreso than while she was in active labor. I could see that the aggressive grunts and movements that the

DANCE DANCE BABY DANCE

choreography called for towards the end weren't just rehearsed anymore.

They were real for her and she used them to expel her pain and get her through the final stretch. I knew I could never complain in front of her again or throw a fit about my sound being off after witnessing her feat, but I didn't have much time to think about the next stage I'd be on because I was too busy making her back it up and dump it one last time into the wheelchair.

All show long I'd been on the side getting her water and ice chips while fanning to make sure she stayed cool. My heart pounded out my chest with the base every time she had to go back out there, but when she was finally done I sighed with relief and tried to rush past everybody not even letting her get changed out of the last costume.

Bianca, who had caught on halfway through the night, was gracious enough to loan us a couple of her police escorts to get through traffic faster. As we thanked her for everything she had already done for us, she wished us well then joined everybody as they put a hand on Tempest's stomach to pray over the safe arrival of the Revival tour's babies.

DANCE DANCE BABY DANCE

It was a fitting name too since it had revived our hope and faith and literally ended with God about to give us the most precious gifts we could ask for. We had went from Tempest and her doctors being surprised she'd gotten pregnant in the first place to almost full term with twins on the road.

According to her it was just more proof that diet played a bigger role with PCOS than people liked to admit because she was already the most fit person I knew. But training for Bianca had came with an energy boosting meal plan to keep them from burning out before the end of the tour and it'd reduced her inflammation and insulin levels. That plus coming home to me shooting up the club every night with no metal detectors on the premises had pretty much guaranteed our outcome.

Tempest had called it on being able to finish the show first since her labor still managed to last almost a full day. By the end she **really** wasn't happy about that though and went back and forth from either telling me how much she loved me to kicking me out the delivery room altogether.

Oh now you don't want to look, huh?

During each of my timeouts I

stayed right outside the door for when she would eventually want me back next to her again and used the time to respond to family and fans who were sending us congrats. The one message that surprised me the most though came from somebody who didn't fit into either category.

We'd ran right into Nat's younger sister Neek on our way out the hotel for the first Atlanta show where she had spoken to me then introduced herself to Tempest as Nakeesha. I wasn't sure if Tempest recognized her or thought she was just another fan, but we never talked about it so I had put it in the back of my mind.

Nat had always been the only person I considered an ex and before Tempest I never even dreamed of having to tell her I was moving on with somebody new so I didn't exactly know what the proper etiquette was. Everything had moved so fast that updating Nat every step of the way could have come off like I was trying to get her attention so I'd avoided reaching out trying to skip over anything that could be misconstrued or perceived as disrespect.

I almost wished I had called though since after catching up with Neek I learned that Nat was doing really good too. She had started grad school and even had a little bump of her own to rub on so I ended the conversation genuinely happy for her. We were each other's first love and backup plan so finally breaking up was tough all around, but there would always be love there from growing up together.

With time and doing things the right way with Tempest I even recognized that I could have been more supportive of Nat when she'd lost the baby. I had used my music as an outlet to heal, but she didn't have anything other than me to lean on. I would never make that mistake again.

TANZANIA GLOVER

When my line was clear again I reached out to my in-laws to make sure that they were safely on the way. Tempest's parents preferred to take the bus from LA instead of the flight like my parents since traveling on short notice was more complicated for them. I'd kept in touch to make sure they were good every step of the way and arranged for DeeDee to pick them up when they made it.

She was anxiously waiting around for her cue to go too since the waiting room had turned into a Smith family reunion down to everybody asking her when it would be her turn to get married and have kids. I'd expected just my immediate family to come through, but since my mama couldn't tell my business from her own they had all rushed to Vegas one by one to witness two new Smiths being added to the tree.

I should have known she would make the birth a family affair though since she hadn't been too happy about us eloping the night before. And for whatever reason she hadn't always been the biggest fan of my relationship anyway, but all it had taken for her to come around and board the Tempest Love Train with everybody else was finding out that she had a grandbaby on the way.

And the second she heard she was getting not one but two, the cold war between my two favorite girls officially ended. She had even made Tempest a copy of our family recipe book which was the biggest step to accepting her and acknowledging us as our own family.

When Tempest called for me to come back to the delivery room for the umpteenth time I saw my younger cousins including Evan who had skipped class to cop a flight from Houston to be here, laughing at me for being a lapdog. He exaggerated as he cracked on me and told them how they should have seen how she'd had me acting on my last tour.

I took it in stride because I knew one day it would be their turn too then thought back to the advice my mama gave whenever any woman asked her the secret to her long marriage.

Don't settle down until you find a man who's scared to tell you no.

She had joked once about me thinking the sun shined out of Tempest's ass, but she honestly wasn't too far off and after watching her soldier through bringing our babies into the world, I was convinced she could do anything.

I had always known her body was capable of greatness, but creating life just took it to another level. It felt like I had witnessed a miracle and I knew neither one of us would ever be the same again. I'd been through this before and there was no crying then so hearing that first whine and the second a couple minutes later as they made their grand entrances into the world brought out the kind of tears that healed from my eyes.

I was scared to hold them. They had already impacted our lives so much, but they were so small I could hold them like a

DANCE DANCE BABY DANCE

football with one hand. I didn't though because I wasn't even confident enough to pick them up while standing.

When it was my turn I took a seat before letting a nurse carefully place them in my arms one after the other like I was a kid being allowed to hold a baby for the first time. Their features were still fresh out the womb and ambiguous, but their gummy wails had them looking like little grumpy, toothless versions of Tempest. She was too out of it to notice, but I couldn't wait to point out that they both already had my ears.

Baby, you know your ears be

giving Keebler sometimes.

Yeah but I bet this elf on a shelf be wearing your ass out.

Black families loved a nickname so we already had everybody calling them Teenie and Tiny, but on paper they would go by Titan Randall and Tiara Ruth Smith.

The hours went by fast, but we got everybody successfully latched on and fed including Tempest who had put me out once before when she smelled food on me since she couldn't have anything but broth all day. DeeDee complained that her sip and see party was basically ruined since almost everybody who would have come was there and had taken a peek before heading out.

One by one the seats in the waiting room became available again as the sun went down, but Tempest's parents still hadn't called. I sent DeeDee and Evan off to the bus station to make sure their phones hadn't died then got right back to being a dad again when I heard a cry. I was a dad.

My mama instinctually jumped up to help when Tempest said she needed to pee, but I let her take over diaper duty instead since I knew I would be knee deep in them at home for the foreseeable future.

"You sure?" she asked us both since she was old school and still couldn't believe I actually wanted to be in the delivery room during the birth.

"Yeah I got her."

I had been man enough to plug it up whenever she let me so I would be man enough to deal with whatever came out. Plus we had been suffocated by doctors, nurses and nosy family all day so we were overdue for a few minutes alone.

"That feel okay?" I asked as I squirted a portable bidet type of thing to soothe the burning sensation the nurse had warned her about.

DANCE DANCE BABY DANCE

Forehead to forehead she sighed and said that it finally felt like her bladder was empty for the first time in months.

"Everything else still hurts though," she weakly chuckled. "I'm really not looking forward to the first poop."

"Wait don't tell me I gotta change your diapers too?" I joked before she cut her eyes. "What? You know I would do it if I had to."

After struggling with the hospital mesh panties and a pad the size of a dinosaur wing we finished up and washed our hands together at the sink, mine under hers to keep her steady on her feet. It reminded me of how we had been in the same position the day before in the hotel, but this time the babies weren't with us.

"Theo, what are you doing?" she whined as I gently swayed with her and hummed in her ear.

"Dancing with my baby, well one of them," I said as I did a fake dip with her.

"Bruh it ain't even been six hours let alone six weeks. Get off me," she joked as she tried to create distance between us.

"Wait it's six weeks now? I thought it was four."

"Minimum six," she corrected, "but we're never

having sex again anyway so you don't have to worry about that," she playfully warned, but I waved her off.

"Nah there's four hands between the two of us *so we gon' be alright*," I rapped while making a tight Black Power fist.

"Please don't make me laugh. It hurts so bad," she groaned and made me get serious again as I wrapped my arms around her from behind.

"It's just for a little while," I said making a promise that I knew for a fact I could keep. She would never have to dance with danger again and her and our babies would always be safe from harm with me. "You're my hero, Temp, you know that?"

"Mm mn. How come all my superpowers do is hurt me? You can keep it."

"So your push presents ain't make it no better?" I asked knowing that she had even more than the new purses she thought she had waiting on her at home.

The few times I'd had to leave her side while on tour I had been setting up big shit for her, the biggest being the remodeling of her dance studio and finishing up the twins' nursery.

"Nope. Fuck you and them bags," she said making me laugh as I checked my back to back dinging phone. Jonathan had finally landed and DeeDee had found Tempest's family out front and they were on their way up. "Alright well I got one more present that'll be here any minute."

Before I could get her back settled good in bed I heard our last visitors talking right before they knocked as they opened the door.

"Either my swaddling skills ain't what they used to be or this girl is already a damned good wiggler," my mama said impressed since Titan was still tucked tightly from the diaper change, but Tiara had stretched and freed herself somehow.

I moved out of the way so Tempest could see her mama and dad in the doorway putting on their facemasks and other PPE as DeeDee wheeled in her Grandma Ruth. I'd met her a few times before, only once on a good day, but that had been more than enough to proudly give my daughter both of her names.

She was a pistol who said what she meant and meant what she said. And before she took anything back she would add more to it. She had even playfully insulted me about being too yellow to join her family then proudly said she wasn't Willy

DANCE DANCE BABY DANCE

Wonka so she didn't have to sugar coat shit. I respected it.

The recognition in her eyes along with her outstretched arms and warm smile let me know she was indeed having a good day and knew she was there to meet her first great-grandchildren.

"Probably both, Chile," she said to my mama as she winked over at a wide smiling Tempest in bed, "but over here we like to call it the sizzle."

TANZANIA GLOVER
FOLLOW ME

Thanks for reading! If you don't want to miss out on any updates about future works of mine then find me on all social media platforms as TanSaidWhat, sign up for my mailing list, and join my reading group Turning The Page With Tanzania Glover.

Visit www.tanzaniaglover.com

And if the cover art took your breath away as much as it did mine, check out the talented artist Dionne Richard! Thank you so much for bringing this couple to life!

DANCE DANCE BABY DANCE THANK YOUS

I said that I was done writing dissertations to my family and friends in this section so I'll try to keep this brief especially since my love for them has remained the same since the first time I did this. But I do want to say that I feel like the luckiest person in the world to be able to go on this journey with people who genuinely love and care for me. Because of the immense amount of love and support that I receive from them, I get to do the thing I love most in the world and I'm forever grateful for it.